Reviews of
Journey Out of Loneliness

Journey Out of Loneliness is beautifully written and masterfully weaves sorrow, joy, suspense, and tender romance throughout the novel. Sit back, get comfortable, and delight in this life-changing mystery. I love it and look forward to the next book in the series!

Terry Beard – Author of *Our Rae of Hope*

Journey Out of Loneliness touched my heart. The author provides character depth, drama, and love. Tragedy invades Missy's life, leaving her to deal with loneliness the best way she knows how. Losing her parents shakes her to the core wondering if she will ever recover. I loved the book and look forward to more from this author.

June Chapko – Author of *The Estate Sale*

Journey Out of Loneliness is an enjoyable read and warm story. It immediately pulled me into the story of a young woman's unique life situation and the suspense surrounding her. Cathey Edgington does a wonderful job weaving faith, love, happiness, and the thread of mystery throughout the story.

Alfred W. Bates – Author of *The Wickie* and *Spirit of the Lighthouse*

Journey Out of Loneliness is for those who enjoy light romantic suspense and stories. The gold in this Christian novel lies in its clearly stated salvation message and in the inspiration given to share that message with the lost. Well done, Cathey Edgington, on a soul-touching debut.

April W. Gardner – Award-Winning Author of *Creek Country Saga*

Journey Out of Loneliness

Journey Out of Loneliness

Cathey Edgington

FRANKLIN
SCRIBES™
PUBLISHERS

Edgington. Cathey
Journey Out of Loneliness
Book One: Faith and Courage series
First Edition
A Novel

Library of Congress Control Number: 2019935969
ISBN Hardback: 978-1-941516-53-9
ISBN Paperback: 978-1-941516-49-2
ISBN eBook: 978-1-941516-50-8

Loneliness—Fiction. 2. Intrigue—Fiction. 3. Suspense—Courage. 4. Faithfulness—Fiction
Scripture taken from the Holy Bible: New International Version. Zondervan, 2015.

Published by Franklin Scribes Publishers.
Franklin Scribes is a registered trademark of Franklin Scribes Publishers.   franklinscribes.com

Contact the author at franklinscribes.com/cathey-edgington
facebook: Cathey Edgington
catheyedgington.wordpress.com

Front book cover by Lisa Edgington of Over the Edge Design.
Cathey Edgington's bio picture: Hair compliments of Stephanie Alejandro of Cyndi's Salon and Spa

This book was printed in the United States of America.

FRANKLIN
SCRIBES™
PUBLISHERS

Dedication

I dedicate this book to my Lord and Savior, Jesus Christ, first. He guided the words written and gave me ideas even in the middle of the night. Writing this book became a therapy helping me get through a very difficult time in my life. I also dedicate it to my small core of friends, Sandy Cleary, Tina McDonald, Nancy Khan, Margaret Latham, and Lila DeVries. They listened to me, let me cry, and comforted me. They helped me with my loneliness.

Acknowledgments

I want to thank Sandy Cleary most of all for telling me to put my story on paper many years ago. She's been my best encourager while I wrote this book. I joined the Christian Writers Group of San Antonio and thank Brenda Blanchard and Allison Pittman who lead the group. I thank the small group of people who critiqued my pages week after week and helped me grow as a writer. Just thinking of myself as a writer is a miracle in itself. Thank you: Sandy Cleary, Al Bates, Terry Beard, Monica Clegg, April Gardner, Jim Hopper, Rebecca Velez, Nancy Christy, Laverne Stanley, and Van Mabrito. I also want to thank the small group of Writers for Him who meet each week for the friendship and critiquing: Sandy Cleary, June Chapko, Terry Beard, Laverne Stanley, and Nancy Christy.

Thank you to Linda Goldfarb for allowing me to mention her Bible Study: *His Warrior Sisters, Owning Christ's Identity* in my book. I had recently completed this study and felt it would be helpful for others to use.

A special thank you to Lisa Edgington of Over the Edge Design, Alissa Edgington, and Rebekah Williams for the book cover. It's perfect.

Prologue

Metal crunching, the thud of the impact, and the sound of a car smashing into a telephone pole filled the air. The last moments flashed through the driver's mind: a truck running a red light, careening toward his car, the bone-cracking jolt of being hit broadside. A few seconds of total silence before bystanders yelled and ran to help. One man pulled out his cell phone and called 911. Another shouted for help to open the car door, so he could see the condition of the passengers.

"Missy...," the woman said faintly from the car.

"I'm a nurse and here to help you, ma'am," the man said, as he reached into the broken window to pat her shoulder and take her pulse. He looked around. "She's going into shock. I need some help here."

Soon the wailing of police and EMS sirens filled the air.

Chapter 1

The morning sun crept over Missy's face waking her with a start. Her pounding heart vibrated in her ears. She looked around remembering she was in her bed and slowly lay back down trying to calm her racing pulse. "That dream again," she muttered to herself. In the dream, as a young girl, she awoke in a strange room feeling very lonely. *It'd been a while since the images invaded my sleep.* She knew the trauma of the last few days had caused its return.

"It's just a dream," she said closing her eyes. *If only the feeling of loneliness didn't leave me feeling so depressed.* The dream didn't trigger her feelings now. She wanted to block out the reasons, but facing what happened to her family caused her dreams. Tomorrow, the reality of the funerals and the loss of her family would leave her feeling alone and would be more unsettling.

I must focus on something else. Missy tried to think of the future. *Four months from today will be my wedding day. I'll become Mrs. Ryan Franklin. It will be the best day of my life, but how can I think of being happy. Marrying the man I love should make me feel whole, but right now, I don't feel whole or happy.*

She tried to envision the day she would become Ryan's wife. It made her sadder, knowing her family wouldn't be there to share it with her. *God will never leave me, nor forsake me.* Her thought brought a timid smile and lifted her spirit, but even the verse couldn't take away the fear of being alone. Missy knew what the dream meant; she was alone for the first time in her life. She didn't know if Ryan would be able to get leave to come home from Iraq. Her best friend, Becky, would be arriving from college sometime today.

"Please, God, let Ryan be here soon. I need him now more than ever. He is—will be— the only family I'll have from now on."

Missy blinked away the tears. So many memories ran through her mind as she looked at pictures on her walls, the trophies on her dresser, and the scrapbook on the nightstand. *When we first moved in, Daddy told me to pick my bedroom even before David could choose his.* She saw the window seat and knew she wanted this room. *How many times have I sat on the window seat and dreamed of what my life could become?*

First, she wanted to be a teacher because of her first-grade teacher, Miss Kelly. Then in sixth grade, an artist, because her picture won a spot in the school art show. Soon her interest switched to music. Playing the flute in junior high inspired her to dream of being part of the symphonic orchestra. As a freshman, after auditioning for a play in drama class, she could see her name in lights on Broadway, but it too faded as other interests took over her life. After graduating from high school, still not knowing what she wanted to do with her life, she started college and got her basics out of the way. Through teaching children in Sunday School at church, she realized God placed a love of children in her heart. Now, in a few months the dream of becoming a teacher would come true. *So many memories. So many dreams.*

Growing up in this house made her very happy. Her parents loved and supported her in anything she wanted to try. Even her brother helped her. Two years older than her, David still took time to encourage her acting by helping her with her lines. She closed her eyes as the tears trickled out and slid down her cheek. David wouldn't be at the wedding nor would her parents. *This is why I dreamed about being very alone.*

The phone rang and jolted Missy out of her memories. She sat straight up, and listened. *I don't want to talk to anyone, especially another reporter. They can leave a message on the answering machine.* She heard a lady's voice. "Hello, I'm calling because I saw the story on the news about the terrible accident which took your parents and brother. I am not a reporter. I need to talk to you about something personal regarding your family. Please call me back . . ." The machine cut off.

Who called? How can I call back if there's not a number? Did this woman know David? Why did the lady's voice sound so familiar? Who is she? I wish I had caller ID, so I could call her back. There was an urgency in the lady's voice, and Missy felt she had to know why the lady called.

Missy placed her feet on the floor and stood. She looked in the mirror and saw her red, puffy, and glazed eyes. "What am I going to do?" she asked her image. She knew only God's strength, not hers, would get her through the coming days, as she faced the most difficult time of her life.

Missy put on her robe and went down the stairs. By the time she reached the last step, memories of her parents and brother overpowered her. The tears came rushing down her face again. *Chai tea!* She had to have some tea to clear her head. She brushed the tears away. *Everything's ready for the funerals, but the lawyer still needs the life insurance policies.* She had to find them.

As she filled the teapot with water, the doorbell rang. "Oh, no, it's starting again," Missy said out loud. *I wish someone was here to answer the door.* She just couldn't face anyone now, not yet.

Then she heard Becky's voice, "Missy, it's me. Are you up yet? I brought breakfast."

Missy exhaled not realizing she'd been holding her breath. She rushed down the hallway to the door and opened it. There stood her best friend, Becky. With tears streaming down her face, she shuttled Becky into the house and shut the door.

Becky wrapped her arms around Missy and held her until she stepped back.

Missy wiped her eyes. "It's so good to see you." She looked out the small window by the door and saw the crowd. "I can't believe how many reporters are out there. I can't face another interview about the accident. They've been hounding me since the news broke about it."

"Your family is important to this town. I'm sorry they're bothering you." Becky saw the look on Missy's face and knew what she had to do. She took Missy's hand and led her to the family room in the back of the house. She gently pushed Missy's shoulder to get her to sit in the easy chair. From a bag which Becky had been holding, she took out a Styrofoam cup of steaming hot Chai tea and a cinnamon roll and placed them on the table beside the chair. "Here, drink your tea and eat your roll. I'll take care of the vultures outside."

Becky went back to the front door. Missy heard her call out to the reporters. "Please leave. My friend needs time right now to come to grips with what's happened to her family. Have some compassion; she just lost her entire family. There's nothing else to report."

Becky closed the door, then leaned on it shaking and whispered, "Father God, help me to help Missy. How can I comfort her at this time? Show me the way, Lord."

Becky walked back to the family room and saw Missy with a slight grin drinking her tea. "What?" she asked, shaking her head. "You know me too well; I take charge then fall apart. You know how hard it is for me to confront them, don't you?"

Missy nodded. "Thank you."

Missy and Becky became friends the day Missy and her family moved into her house. She smiled thinking of memories of the first day. Becky came to the door even before the moving vans were completely unloaded. She held two baby dolls in her arms and gave one to Missy. From then on, they did everything together until college. Becky won a full scholarship to college in Denton, Texas, and Missy won a scholarship at Midwestern State University. Even miles apart, they kept in touch daily.

"When you were yelling at the reporters, did you see a black pickup?"

"Yes, I did. Why?" Becky asked.

"I've seen the truck there every day since the accident," Missy replied. "I keep thinking it's just another reporter, but it remained there last night after all the other news vans were gone."

"How do you know?"

"I had a hard time sleeping last night. So, about one this morning, I got up and came downstairs to get some warm milk. I looked out the window by the front door and saw the truck. A man sat in the front seat looking at something on what looked like an iPad. I saw his profile by the light of the screen."

"Maybe you should call the police."

"I will. After the accident, Chief Stone told me to call him at any time, but right now, I just want to hear what's happening with you."

Becky nodded and began telling Missy about her

classes and the people she'd met this year at college.

While Becky rattled on, Missy thought again about the years they'd been like sisters. Just listening to her friend made her feel better. *She always seemed to know my thoughts before me. I need Becky by my side tomorrow.*

Becky stopped talking and noticed the pain on Missy's face. *I wish I could take away her pain, but I know only God can remove Missy's pain.* "I'll be here to help you through tomorrow."

"I know." Missy tucked her feet under her. She leaned her head back and closed her eyes. The silence between them left Missy relaxed and feeling more comfortable knowing someone else was in the house. Soon she drifted off.

Chapter 2

The ringing phone made Missy jump. *Where did Becky go, and how long have I been asleep?* Then she heard the voice of the lady who called earlier. She struggled to get up, but her leg tingled with numbness and she couldn't stand. *Did I dream Becky was here?* At the sound of footsteps, Missy called out, "Pick up the phone." Too late, the machine cut off.

Becky walked into the family room with a quizzical look on her face. "Did you recognize the caller?" she asked.

"No, I don't think so, but it's the second time she's called today. Her voice seems so familiar. I wonder if she's someone who knows... knew David." Missy stammered.

"Well, she didn't leave a number, so how can you call her back?"

"I don't know. I need to buy a new answering machine with caller ID," Missy said more to herself than to Becky.

"Are you ready to get dressed?" Becky picked up the cold cup of tea and uneaten cinnamon roll.

"I guess. How long did I asleep?

"About an hour." Missy followed her friend to the kitchen. "You didn't sleep much last night, did you?"

"No. I had the nightmare again."

"The one you kept having when you were little?" Becky put the cup in the sink and the cinnamon roll in a storage bag.

"Yes. I guess an empty house caused the dream to resurface."

"Well, I'm here now and I'm not leaving for a few days." Becky looked at Missy. "While you were asleep, I put my suitcase in the guest room. I told my parents I'm staying here until I go back to college. I hope it's okay."

"Yes. You are a true friend. I know your home is just next door, but it'll be nice having someone in the house with me. Thank you." Missy reached out and took Becky's hand. "I seem to be repeating myself a lot since you got here, but I can't tell you how much it means to have you here with me." She looked down the hallway toward the front door. "Is the black truck still out there?"

"Yes, it is. I was looking out the window upstairs when the phone rang." Becky squeezed Missy's hands, "So, you need to call the chief about it. I'm glad I'm staying with you in case something dangerous is going on. You hear about it all the time; homes being broken into when there's a death in the family." Becky looked Missy in the eye and cleared her throat. "Have you heard from Ryan? Do you know if he's on his way home yet?"

"No, I haven't heard anything from him." Tears slipped down Missy's face. "I do hope the message from the Red Cross got through to him. I tried calling his cell phone but couldn't connect. I don't know exactly where he is because of security in the war zone. Oh, Becky, I can't lose him too." She fell into Becky's arms and cried.

Becky rubbed Missy's back. "Have faith, God will keep him safe for you."

"Faith is about all I have left." Missy stepped back and reached for a tissue. "I have to keep repeating the verse in the Bible, 'I will never leave you nor forsake you.'" Missy threw the tissue in the trash. "But it's not helping. I need Ryan to hold me and help me through this right now. Don't get me wrong, it's great having you here, but I need him beside me today and especially tomorrow. Do you think he'll come?"

"If Ryan got the message, he'll do everything in his power to get home to you. I know how much he loves you." Becky stroked Missy's blond hair and rubbed her shoulders. "Okay, how about a nice hot soaking bath to relieve the tension I feel in your shoulders. I'll get it ready while you go pick out what you'll wear today. Okay?"

Missy nodded. "Thank you, again"

* * *

As Becky filled the tub with bubble bath, Missy looked bewildered as she entered the bathroom carrying two blouses. Taking the blouses, Becky said, "Here, let me pick out something for you. Get in the tub and relax."

Missy couldn't think straight and did things on auto pilot. She didn't want to make any decisions, and it helped so much having her friend take control.

Emerging from the bathroom some time later in her bathrobe, Missy stood by her bed in deep thought for a moment and stared at the clothes laid out for her.

Becky saw the worry lines on Missy's brow. "What are you thinking about?" She picked up the pants and handed them to her troubled friend.

"I've been thinking about the lady who called. I think I know her."

"Where do you know her from?" Becky asked.

"I don't know, but there's something in her voice telling me I need to talk to her."

"Well, when she calls again, I'll make sure you get to speak to her. Okay? Get dressed. I'll be in the guest room," Becky said over her shoulder as she left the room.

Missy nodded and started dressing. "What if she doesn't call again?"

"She will. I heard it in her voice; talking to you is as important to her as it is to you." Becky walked back to Missy's bedroom door but stopped in the hallway. "You said her voice is familiar. Could she be a relative?"

"No, both Momma and Daddy were only children, and all my grandparents are gone." After slipping on the blouse, Missy stepped into the hallway. "I don't have any relatives left."

"We'll just have to wait until she calls again to find out." Becky put her hand on Missy's shoulder. "Is there anything that needs to be done for tomorrow? Do you need to go to the funeral home or has everything been taken care of?"

"The funeral plans are in place, but the lawyer called asking for the life insurance policies. He needs to begin the process, so the insurance will cover the funerals." Missy wrung her hands while looking toward her parents' bedroom. "Will you please help me go through Daddy's desk and files? I'd rather not do it alone."

Becky nodded and put an arm around her friend's shoulders as she walked with her to the master bedroom.

Missy wasn't sure of her financial situation. Tears clouded her eyes again, but she blinked them away. *I can do all things through Christ who strengthens me. Lord, I need your strength now. Help me cope while going through Momma and Daddy's things.*

Becky's voice echoed Missy's thoughts. "'I can do all things through Christ who strengthens me.' Lean on God's promises. You'll get through this. I'll be here with you until Ryan arrives."

Missy nodded and, together, they entered her parents' bedroom. "I have no idea where to start looking… maybe in the desk." She went to the desk in the corner of the big master bedroom, sank into the leather chair, and absorbed the feel and smell of her dad's scent. She found it comforting.

Missy took a deep breath and pulled out the center drawer. "Daddy always kept everything orderly and often said, 'There's a place for everything and everything has a place.' Do you know how many times he told me this while looking at my room during my teenage years?"

"You weren't the neatest person back then. You're better at it now." Becky chuckled.

"I always picked everything up, but in no time, it became messy again. We had an ongoing battle about my bedroom being neat. I wonder why I didn't inherit his trait of neatness. I had to work hard at keeping my room clean."

"We don't always get the good traits from our parents." Becky held up a photograph. "Y'all look so happy in this picture."

Missy rose from the chair and took the picture from Becky. "This picture is the last of our family together." A tear ran down her cheek.

"I still don't know where you got your beautiful blonde hair," Becky mused. "Your mom had auburn hair and your dad had hair black as night. Even David had dark curly hair."

"Momma always said I got it from my grandmother who had very blonde hair. I never really thought about it." Missy traced each face in the portrait with her finger. "We were so happy when this picture was taken at David's graduation in his cap and gown." She returned the picture to Becky and wiped her eyes. "Well, I guess I've put this off long enough. I need to get into their files now."

Missy moved back to the desk and opened the right-hand drawer where she knew her dad stored some of the important papers. She started leafing through the files which were arranged in alphabetical order and stopped at a file labeled: David. She pulled it out and found his birth certificate, high school diploma, programs with awards which David received, and a copy of his college diploma. "My parents were so proud when David graduated from college *magnum cum laude*. I heard Daddy say to David 'Never thought you could make me prouder, son, but you have by this achievement.' Momma and Daddy always expressed how very proud they were of us in everything we did, but the look on Daddy's face at David's graduation, radiated pure love and pride."

Missy put the file back in the drawer and found a file with her name on it. She pulled it out expecting to find the same type of things which were in David's file. Everything was there – her high school diploma, programs from shows she participated in, awards ceremonies, and other memorabilia, except her birth certificate.

She continued looking though the drawer and didn't see anything the lawyer needed. She tried to pull out the left side drawer, but it was locked. She looked at Becky and then back at the drawer. "I wonder where the key is."

Becky started sorting through things on the desk while Missy checked the center drawer.

"Do you think your dad would carry it on his key chain?" Becky asked.

"I don't know. The bag of personal effects the hospital gave me is in my room. I haven't looked through it yet. Would you go look, please?"

"Sure." Becky turned to walk out of the bedroom but paused. "Where in your room? I didn't see any bags when I selected your clothes."

"I stuffed the bags in the window seat storage. It's always been my hiding place for important things. I couldn't look at them at the time."

"Okay, be right back."

Missy picked up her dad's favorite ink pen and the paperweight she made when she was eight. *I sure do miss you, Daddy.*

Becky returned to the room carrying three plastic pouches. "Your mom's purse is in this one, but I'm not sure which bag has your dad's things."

Missy took the bags, laid one on the desk, and handed the other one back to Becky. "This one belongs to Daddy. See, his initials are on the wallet. I gave it to him for Christmas." She wiped away some tears. "Please take the keys out for me."

Becky opened the bag, pulled out the key ring with multiple keys, and started to hand them to her friend.

Missy held up her hands. "No, you try it, my hands are shaking so bad I wouldn't be able to open the drawer if there was only one key to try."

Becky looked at the keys and saw one for a house, a car, what looked to be the office door, and two smaller ones. She walked behind the desk to try the smallest one. It worked. She pulled the drawer open and stepped back.

"This is probably where Daddy keeps the bank account information and checkbook." Missy found the bank file and pulled out the statements. "Well, it looks like Daddy's salary as the bank president was more than I thought. Look at this last entry as 'salary deposit.'"

"I wonder if he did any investing? It's something the lawyer will need to know if he doesn't already."

"I see a payment to American Funds, so I bet Daddy has all the information in this drawer." Missy replaced the bank statements and saw the file labeled: Insurance Policies. She pulled the file out and found the policies inside. One for her dad, mother, David, and one on herself. She opened hers first. Why, she didn't know. *The policy is for five hundred thousand dollars.* "Wow!"

Becky leaned over to look, "Wow, is right. Did you know they had a policy on you?"

"Yes, but I didn't know the amount. Most families focus on the parents, so the children would have money when needed."

"What kind of policies did they have on

themselves and David?"

Missy opened the policy with her dad's name on it and gasped. "Two million dollars." She looked wide-eyed at Becky who nodded toward the other two files. Slowly, Missy opened the file with her mother's name. "One million." *Unbelievable.* She opened David's file and saw five hundred thousand, the same as her policy. Tears ran down her face as she blinked at Becky and inhaled. "Well, I don't think I'll have to worry about money."

Becky took the files and spread them out on the desk. "They really made provisions in case something happened. Your dad's policy lists the beneficiaries as your mom, then the amount would be split between you and David. Your mom's is divided the same way, but David's lists only you as the beneficiary. I wonder why your parents didn't have themselves on the policy?"

Missy shrugged and looked through the other files in the drawer. "I don't see a file for American Funds."

"There should be something which shows what kind of accounts he invested in and the account balance."

"Wait. I remember Daddy showing David a file cabinet in the back of their closet. He said there were important papers in it." Missy stood, headed to the closet door, turned on the light, and suddenly stopped. With a sob in her voice, "I can't do this. It smells like Momma's rose scent she always wore."

"I know this is very hard for you right now, but it must be done. I'm here with you." Becky placed her hand on her friend's shoulder. "Do you want me to get the files and bring them to you?"

"Yes, please. I can't go in the closet right now."

"Go sit down and I'll get what files I think may be important."

Missy stood next to the windows watching the reporters out by the street and realized the black truck wasn't at the curb. *I hope I don't see it again.*

Becky walked out of the closet. "The file cabinet is locked, so one of those keys must open it."

Missy picked up the keys from the desk, handed them to Becky, and watched her go back into the closet. Reseating herself, she heard the drawers open and knew the right key had been found.

Becky returned with a sealed envelope and handed it to Missy. "This has your name on it."

She looked at Becky with questioning eyes. On the front of the envelope, she saw *Melissa* written on it. Missy nodded.

Becky raised her eyebrows. "You want me to open it?"

"Yes, I'm afraid."

"Why?"

"I don't really know, but something tells me it's important. I don't trust my mind to understand things right now. So, I'm relying on you to tell me what it is. Okay?"

Becky took the envelope, broke the seal,

removed the papers, and started scanning them. Her eyes pooled with tears, and she shook her head.

"What is it?" Missy asked with a trembling voice.

"It's your adoption papers."

"What?" Missy stood and took the papers from Becky. On the first page, the name *Melissa Powers* was written in bold print. "I was adopted? I had a different last name?"

Becky touched her friend's shoulder. "They didn't tell you?"

Missy sank into the chair. "I had no idea. I would've told you if I knew." Missy stared at the papers silently and shook her heard. "Momma and Daddy didn't say anything to even make me *think* I was adopted. I felt loved and they treated me just like David. I wonder if he knew?"

"If they adopted you as a baby, maybe he didn't know."

"Maybe, but..." Missy scrunched up her face.

"What?"

"You know I don't have any memories earlier than moving into this house when I was three years old," Missy told her friend. "Which leaves some missing years. Why don't I remember anything about where we lived before here?"

"You were young. I don't remember where I lived at three years old." Becky chuckled. "No, I take it back, I've lived in the same house all my life until I went away to college. Maybe you were too young to remember anything different."

The phone rang. Missy looked at Becky and then the phone. "Answer it, please," Missy begged.

Becky lifted the handset. "Hello."

"Oh, hello. Missy?" the caller inquired.

"No, I'm a friend. Can I help you?" Becky pointed and silently mouthed, "It's her."

Missy's eyes grew wide and she rolled her hand in a circle, beckoning her friend to continue with the call.

"Is there a message I can give her for you?" Becky put the phone on speaker.

"Missy doesn't know me, well...not exactly, but I need to talk to her, to see her face to face if she will let me."

"Why?" Becky asked.

"Well, I have some information about her family."

"I'm sorry, but if you saw the news, you'd know her family was killed in a terrible accident. She doesn't need reporters questioning her right now." Becky shook her head.

"I'm not . . . I'm not a reporter, I promise. I'm sorry. I'm not handling this very well. You see, when I saw her picture during her interview, I knew God led me to watch the news, so I'd see her."

"What do you mean?" Becky looked at Missy and mouthed, "Do you believe her?"

Missy nodded with tears in her eyes.

"Well, if I could see Missy and talk with her in

person, she'd understand," the lady continued.

"Why does it have to be in person? Why can't you talk to her on the phone and explain yourself?"

"Well, I know she's hurting right now and feeling all alone, but it's very important I meet her face to face. I don't think what I have to tell her would be believed over the phone."

"Why?"

"Well, it's . . . it's complicated and if we can meet, everything will become clear."

Becky looked at Missy and said into the phone, "What if I meet you first and you explain it to me."

"I guess . . . ah . . . okay, if you think it would help you believe what I have to say to her. Once we meet, you'll understand why I need to see her. Can you meet me in an hour? What is your name?"

"My name is Becky Thomas and I'm a very good friend of Missy. I'd do anything to help her get through this right now." Becky mouthed, "Is it okay?"

Missy nodded.

"I don't want to add to her burdens if this turns out to be nothing of importance." Becky smiled at her friend.

"This is very important. If you feel you need to meet me first and let me explain things to you for Missy's sake, I'll do what you ask. How about we meet at Trudy's Coffee Shop by the university in about an hour? Do you know it?"

"Yes, I do. Trudy knows me, and I'll feel comfortable meeting you there. How will I know you?"

"I'll tell Trudy I'm expecting you. Okay?"

"Okay, bye." Becky hung up the phone and turned to Missy. "What do you think?"

"I don't know, but I feel this is God helping me. I have goose bumps all over." Missy rubbed her arms. "There's something about her voice, but I can't put my finger on it. Thank you, Becky, for doing this for me."

"No problem but call Chief Stone now about the guy in the truck and this phone call. I don't want to leave you alone if some lunatic is out front watching you."

"Okay, I'll call right now." Missy picked up the phone.

Chapter 3

One hour later, Becky walked into Trudy's Coffee Shop. She scanned the people seated at the tables but didn't know who to look for. She turned to the counter and smiled at Trudy. "Hello, Trudy. I'm supposed to meet someone here."

"Hi, Becky." Trudy smiled and pointed toward the back of the café. "The lady in the last booth with her back to us said she is waiting for you."

Becky nodded. When she reached the lady, she stopped, eyes widened, and felt light headed as though she might faint. Becky saw a lady who was the spitting image of Missy. She blinked not believing her eyes. "Who . . . are . . . you?"

"Please sit down and let me explain. You're Becky, right?"

Becky only nodded as she slid into the seat across from the mystery lady.

"As I said on the phone," she began, "you'd have to meet me to understand. My name is Cassandra or Cissy as some call me. As you can see, I look like Missy."

Becky nodded, opened her mouth to say something but couldn't form any words.

"Our story is a long one. I want to tell it to you, but I'd rather you both hear it at the same time."

"You . . . you look exactly like Missy."

"Well, it's because she's my twin sister."

Becky couldn't speak for a few moments. She searched the lady's face for the truth. The same blonde hair, eyes blue as a Texas sky, and when the lady grinned, which mirrored Missy's grin. Becky knew she was telling the truth.

Becky took out her phone. "Let me call Missy and see if she'll meet you."

"Thank you," Cissy said with a sigh of relief.

"Wow, now I know why Missy kept saying your voice sounded familiar. You sound just like her when you said, 'Thank you' just now." With tears in her eyes, Becky called Missy.

Missy answered after the first ring. "Hello."

"What if I had been a reporter?" Becky admonished.

"Well, you're not. Who is she? How do I know her?"

"Missy, take a deep breath and slow down." Becky heard Missy inhale then continued. "First, is the patrol car the chief sent over still outside?"

"Yes, the patrol car is still parked at the curb."

"Okay, good. Are you up to having some company now?"

"Do I want to have company?" asked Missy.

"Yes, you do indeed." Becky grinned at Cissy. "Be there in a few minutes."

"Great, bye." Missy's hand shook as she replaced the phone in the cradle.

* * *

Missy raced to her room and looked at herself in the mirror. She couldn't remember what she'd put on after her bath. She brushed her hair and gathered it in the back with a clip. Looking at her eyes, she saw their redness from crying. She went to the bathroom, ran cold water on a wash cloth, and pressed it to her eyes. *Ah, it feels so good.* She applied a little makeup although she really didn't need it. *Why do I feel so giddy? I feel like I did on my birthday as a child, trying hard to be calm while waiting to receive my presents. Could this lady be someone who knows about my adoption and where I came from?*

She ran downstairs and peeked out the side window by the door. She paced from the kitchen to the front door and back again. Another glance out the window. *How long does it take to drive from Trudy's? Ten minutes? Why aren't they here yet? It's been thirty minutes since Becky called.*

The black truck was back, parked in front of the patrol car so she felt safe. She decided to make some tea to stop the jitters. At the sound of a car door shutting, she stopped filling the tea kettle. She hurried down the hall to the front door and opened it before Becky had a chance to ring the bell. Missy looked outside over Becky's shoulders and then back to Becky. "Where's my company?"

Becky turned Missy around, closed the door, and guided her to the family room and instructed, "Sit down."

Missy sat but with a puzzled look on her face. Before she could say anything, the doorbell rang.

Becky held up her hand. "Stay right there. I'll get the door."

Missy heard the door open then muted giggles and whispered voices coming down the hallway. Not one voice, but several. Her curiosity heightened, but she remained seated. Becky entered the room with others behind her. Missy stood only to sink back into the chair. Four ladies stood there, and one looked exactly like her.

The one who looked like her approached. "Missy, I'm Cassandra, your twin sister."

Missy's eyes grew wide and pooled with tears. "I don't . . . how . . . what happened?"

Cassandra knelt next to Missy's chair and pointed to the others. "We're here to tell you our story. These are our sisters, Dotty, Joy, and Gayle."

Missy looked at all of them and then back at Cassandra. "What do you mean? My sisters—my twin?"

Becky came forward and laid a hand on Missy's shoulder. "Remember all of those dreams you had when you were young?"

Missy nodded.

"Well, they weren't exactly dreams. You were

remembering things which happened when you were younger—before you came to live in this house."

"I know this is a shock, especially after your loss, but we've been searching for you for years," Dottie said. The others nodded in agreement.

"Maybe you should start from the beginning." Becky motioned for everyone to take a seat on the couch and chairs around the room.

Cassandra pulled a chair close to Missy's and took her hand as she looked at the others. "Dottie, maybe you should start, since you remember more than the rest of us."

Dottie nodded and took a deep breath. "Where do I begin? I am the oldest, next is Joy, Gayle, and then you and Cassandra or Cissy as we call her. You were always Missy. We lived not far from here as a matter of fact, but as some would say, 'on the other side of the tracks.'"

Missy shook her head. "In this town?"

"Yes." Dottie continued. "Daddy died in a car accident when you and Cissy were about two and a half. We didn't have much money even when Daddy was alive and working. Momma was a proud woman and didn't ask for anything for herself, but always tried to give us what we needed. After Daddy died, Momma started working two jobs just to keep a roof over our heads and food on the table."

"I don't remember anything." Missy shook her head.

"Eighteen years have passed, and you were very

young." Dottie shook her head. "We wore hand-me down clothes which usually came from the church, but Momma always made us a special dress on our birthdays. On Christmas, Momma made sure we had a doll or something we wanted. We were loved very much."

Cissy broke in and squeezed Missy's hand. "We only had each other back then."

"When I was fifteen, and you and Cissy were three, I took care of all of you during the summer while Momma worked." Dottie smiled at the others. "She did housekeeping for a couple of families and worked in a café as a waitress at night. School would be starting soon, and I'd have to quit school to stay home with you two so Momma could work."

"There wasn't money for a sitter." Cissy explained.

"Momma felt bad about it and started working a third job doing sewing for a company, so she could afford someone to watch you while the rest of us were in school." A sadness washed over Dottie's face. "Well, after about four months with Momma working all the jobs, she became run down and very tired. I told her to quit working so hard because I didn't mind staying with you two. Momma said I needed an education, so I wouldn't find myself in her situation of working dead-end jobs."

Tears ran down Missy's cheeks. "What happened?"

"Momma continued working and didn't sleep

much." Dottie paused and took a deep breath. "Well, one night in late January, after I had put you and Cissy in bed and the others were doing their homework, someone knocked on the door. Momma always told me not to answer. So, I sent Joy and Gayle into our bedroom, and I stayed in the kitchen so if anyone looked in the window, they wouldn't see us. Then I heard a woman say, 'Please open the door, we're from the police. We know you are in there. It's about your mother.'"

Missy gasped. "Oh no."

"I hurried to the door and opened it. A woman and a policeman stood on the front porch. She explained there'd been an accident and the EMS took Momma to the hospital. The policeman asked if there were any grandparents, aunts, or uncles who could be called about the situation. I just shook my head not knowing what to say."

"We had no other relatives?" Missy asked.

"No one. They kept talking and asking questions, but I didn't hear everything because all I could think about was Momma. 'Not Momma,' I said out loud and then I tried to think who to call. The only person who ever helped us was the pastor at church. I told them his name and which church. The policeman wrote down the information and nodded to the lady as he went to the police car. By this time, Joy and Gayle came into the room. I told them to make sure you two were asleep."

Joy smiled at Missy. "We were listening at the

bedroom door, so we knew what had happened."

"When they returned, we hugged each other." Dottie looked at Joy and Gayle. "We'd gone through this before when Daddy died, but Momma knew what to do and held us together. I could only think 'This couldn't be happening again.' The woman said I could go to the hospital to be with Momma, and she would stay with the rest of you. I didn't know her and knew if y'all woke up, you'd be scared, so I told her to take Joy and Gayle to be with Momma. I would stay with the two of you."

"We were still sleeping?" Missy asked.

"Yes, once you two were in bed, you both slept soundly." Dottie smiled and continued, "The woman finally agreed, but before they could leave, the policeman came back inside with the pastor and his wife. I knew by the look on their faces Momma had died. The pastor's wife took Joy and Gayle into the kitchen. The policeman sat down and told me he just got word Momma died of a head injury. It seemed she'd hit an icy patch on the road and loss control of the car. She ran into a tree while trying to regain control." Dottie wiped away tears.

Missy wiped tears from her eyes, also. "I don't remember her, but I feel a hurt in my heart."

"I couldn't cry then. I guess I was in shock," Dottie explained. "I only stared at the pastor and asked 'Why?' He tried to comfort me, but I couldn't stop thinking of what would happen to the five of us. Finally, I voiced the question. The pastor and policeman looked at the woman, who I found out later, worked for the Child Protection Agency. Her name was Mrs. Reed; she seemed very kind."

"We felt differently about her later," Gayle inserted.

"Mrs. Reed told me she'd have to take us to a shelter. I asked, 'Tonight?' and she just nodded. I didn't even have the strength to protest. She told us to gather some clothes for all of us. The pastor and the policeman carried you both to the car. You didn't even wake up. We were put in a temporary home for the night."

"Were we all together?" Missy asked.

"No. You and Cissy weren't allowed to stay with us." Dottie clasped and unclasped her hands. "I was told you woke up the next morning, screaming, and wouldn't let Mrs. Reed touch you because you didn't know her. I'm sorry I couldn't be with you when you woke up. I know you were scared."

Becky and Missy exchanged glances knowing this sounded like Missy's nightmare—waking up in a strange place and not knowing the people around her.

Cissy squeezed her twin's hand again. "You had bad dreams too, didn't you?"

Missy nodded, unable to speak.

"My nightmare consisted of missing a part of myself," Cissy said, "and now I know, I was missing you."

Tears flowed from Missy's eyes as she slowly looked from one sister to another. "What happened to us?"

Dottie glanced at her other sisters. "Mrs. Reed told me since there wasn't a kinship home for all of us to be placed in and no foster home could take all five of us, we were going to three different homes."

"What's a kinship home?" Missy asked.

"Mrs. Reed told me a kinship home is with a relative. She said she knew of a couple of families waiting to adopt a little girl but not two. I tried to tell her we needed each other and needed to stay together. I could take care of all of us, but she kept saying she was the professional and knew the best situation for us. I guess we were all still in shock, because by the time I understood what was happening and demanded to see someone about our rights, you two had already been placed with a family for adoption, and no one would tell me where."

"We were all in shock; it happened so fast." Joy wiped a tear from her cheek.

"You couldn't see us?" Missy asked.

"No. Mrs. Reed kept saying 'according to law, the adoptions are sealed, and no one can know the information.' We felt lost not knowing what to do." Dottie smiled at her sisters. "Joy, Gayle, and I were sent to different foster homes, but were able to keep in touch. We never knew where y'all were living." Dottie paused and wiped the tears off her face.

"This happened eighteen years ago, and not a day went by we didn't look at everyone we passed hoping to find you," Joy exclaimed.

"It seems unfair not to be able to see each other." Missy shook her head.

"Yes, it was, but we kept looking for both of you." Gayle smiled.

"As years passed, I graduated from high school, got a scholarship, went to college, and majored in law," Dottie continued. "I wanted to know what could be done to find you. Then, one day, about a year ago, while at the public library, Cissy walked in with some of her friends. My heart raced as I watched her. I had to make sure I had the right person and when one of her friends called her Cassandra, I knew." Dottie looked lovingly at her sister.

"When I heard Dottie say 'Cissy,' I turned and came face to face with my past. I knew she was talking to me because my heart started pounding." Cissy smiled. "I remember Mrs. Reed said my name could never be taken away from me. But I knew, Cassandra didn't sound right. When Dottie called me Cissy, I knew why."

"She came straight into my arms and we hugged." Dottie sniffled. "Her friends were confused especially when she introduced me as her sister. They just looked at us like we were crazy. I called Joy and Gayle immediately and they met us at my house."

"We talked late into the night, completely losing track of time when we realized it was after eleven," Cissy continued the story. "I panicked knowing my parents would be worried sick. I called them and explained everything and asked them to come pick me up. When my parents arrived, they immediately saw the truth in what I'd told them." Cissy smiled. "Because as you can see, we all resemble each other."

Missy glanced from one sister to the other and nodded. *I feel a peace only God can give; I have a family again, and they love me.*

"My parents told me I'd been adopted, but I didn't know I had any relatives," Cissy commented. "My adoptive parents are wonderful, and they encouraged me to get to know my sisters. We held sleepovers at Dottie's house, talking all night long to catch up on the seventeen years apart." She looked at her oldest sister. "Dottie's married to a lawyer. She met him while doing her internship. Oh, she's a lawyer, too and a very good one."

Dottie blushed.

"Joy is married, too, and is the mother of a little boy, Daniel." Cissy giggled. "We're aunts. Gayle is engaged to Tyler Hughes, a serviceman stationed in Iraq, and he's due to return next month, and they're getting married then."

Missy caught her breath and looked down with tears dripping onto her clutched hands.

Becky squeezed Missy's shoulder. "Missy's engaged to a serviceman too, Ryan, but hasn't heard from him in quite a while. She sent a message to him about the accident, but so far hasn't heard if he's coming home."

"The military system doesn't always work the way we want it to," Gayle explained. "I'm sure your fiancé will call as soon as he's able."

The flood gates opened, and Missy started sobbing.

"I'm so sorry for the loss of your family and the uncertainty of when Ryan is going to return." Cissy tipped Missy's head back up. "You didn't know you were adopted, did you?"

Missy shook her head. She reached for a tissue, wiped the tears, and cleared her throat. "Becky had just opened an envelope which held my adoption papers, right before you called the last time. I didn't remember anything before moving into this house with my parents and brother."

"God sometimes works in mysterious ways. You do believe in God, don't you?" Cissy asked.

Missy nodded. "Without the love of Jesus Christ, I don't know how I would've gotten through this week. I know God is with me during this time."

"I don't usually watch the news, but when I turned the television on this morning, the news was on." Cissy looked around the room. "Before I could switch channels, your image appeared on the screen. I did a double take and called Dottie to tell her to turn on the news. She was laughing when she answered, and I asked, 'What's so funny?' The only thing she said, 'We found Missy.'"

Dottie chimed in. "We'd told Cissy about you but didn't know where you were or if we'd ever see you again. We've been praying so very long and finding Cissy was an answer to our prayers. I guess we didn't have enough faith God would give you back to us as well. I decided Cissy needed to contact you to break the news in hopes your twin connection would kick in and make this easier on you."

Everyone looked at Missy and didn't say anything for a few seconds. Then Missy asked, "Am I dreaming again?"

"No, sweetie." Becky comforted. "God sent you the answers to your prayers."

"What prayers?" Missy asked.

"To fill the loneliness you've always felt even though you had a wonderful supportive family. Your sisters missing from your life caused the loneliness."

"Being here with my sisters makes me feel complete," Missy said. "How could I have blocked all of this—all of you—from my memory?"

"Missy, when Daddy died, it was really hard on you," Dottie explained. "You didn't understand and couldn't be left alone at all. One of us always had to be with you and this lasted for months. Then one day you told me you had to put your friend to bed because she was sick. I asked you what friend. You told me, 'My friend whose daddy died.' Then you went into your room by yourself for the first time since Daddy's death. I peeked in, saw you holding a doll, and rocking her back and forth. You told your doll 'It's okay, Kathie, your daddy's in heaven with Jesus, and He's watching over you.' I knew then you heard everything I said regarding death and heaven as I'd told you the same thing."

"I had a baby doll named Kathie?" Missy sighed.

Dottie nodded. "Momma couldn't talk about Daddy's death and didn't know how to deal with trying to help us understand. I asked my Sunday school teacher, Mrs. Rose, about death and she helped me, and I helped all of you."

"When Mrs. Reed told you about Momma, I guess you blocked everything from your mind instead of dealing with another loss." Cissy gently patted her twin's hand.

Missy looked at her sisters and then at Becky. "I'm overwhelmed with all of this— all of you. So much information. My thoughts are swirling around. I can't even think of questions to ask."

"Missy would you like to lay down for a little while?" Becky said. "You've had two big shocks today and maybe you need time to process all this information."

"No!" Missy stood. "I don't want any of you to leave me. I might not see you again." Tears poured down her face.

Cissy stood and gently touched Missy's cheek with a tissue to wipe away her tears. "We aren't going anywhere. If you want to lie down, I'd be happy to sit with you while you sleep." She smiled and looked at her oldest sister then back at her twin. "I just remembered doing the same thing when we were little. Whenever we got in trouble, Missy, you were the one who always cried yourself to sleep. I'd just sit and hold your hand. You were the tenderhearted one. Now I know how much I've missed you."

The twins looked at each other and, in an instant, they embraced. After a while, Missy pulled away and smiled at her other sisters and opened her arms to them. They were in a group hug when the doorbell rang.

"I'll answer the door," Becky announced. She doubted if any of the sisters heard her.

The group hugged Missy one at a time and told her how much she'd been missed. They all talked at the same time—stopped—laughed—and cried together.

"We need another sleepover, just to catch up." Cissy laughed.

Becky returned to the family room and watched them from the doorway not wanting to interrupt the family moment. She caught Missy's eye and smiled.

Missy reached out her hand to her dear friend. "Becky's always been a sister to me and she needs to be in our group hug."

They all gathered together again with arms around one another and tears of joy in all their eyes.

As everyone released each other, Missy asked, "Who was at the door?"

"Some ladies from the church brought sandwich fixings," Becky replied. "They only wanted to drop off the food and offer their condolences. I thanked them for you; they said they'd be back tomorrow with more food. I hope it's okay?"

Missy nodded.

"Do you want to lie down now?" Becky touched

her friend's shoulder.

Missy shook her head and glanced at the clock. "I can't. Look at the time. The lawyer will be here any minute, and I haven't found the investment file to give him."

"Don't worry about it right now." Becky squeezed Missy's hand. "You found the life insurance policies, and the lawyer said he had the wills. The rest can be taken care of later. You need to rest since you didn't sleep much last night. I don't know how you'll get through tomorrow unless you get some sleep."

Cissy stepped forward. "Missy, I know you don't know me, yet, but I'd be happy to help in any way needed. I'm sure Dottie, Joy, and Gayle would too. If it's okay with you, we want to be with you tomorrow at the funeral."

"Oh, yes. Please come, it would mean so much to me." Missy wiped tears off her cheeks. "In a way, it's as if God is giving me a family just when I need it most. I loved my parents and brother so much. They were the only family I remember. Please sit with me tomorrow."

"Thanks to God, Missy will have family with her tomorrow besides people from the church and me." Becky smiled.

The doorbell rang again, and Becky went to answer it expecting reporters, but when she opened the door, a young man stood on the porch.

"May I help you?" Becky asked.

The man handed her a card which read Richard

Jameson, Attorney at Law. "I'm here to speak with Missy Calhoun. I'm from her lawyer's office."

"Come in." Becky motioned him inside. She looked to see if the reporters had left but a few remained. News vans lined the street as did the black truck and patrol car. Becky offered the lawyer her hand and said, "I'm Becky Thomas, Missy's friend. She's in the family room." She gestured toward her right. "If you'd wait in the living room for a moment, I'll get her."

The lawyer nodded and entered the room.

Becky returned to the family room and handed Missy the card. "He says he's from your lawyer's office," Becky whispered. "He's younger than I expected."

"Mr. Sims did call to tell me he'd send someone over to pick up the policies." Missy indicated the card. "This is from the lawyer's office." She turned to her sisters. "I'll be right back."

Becky and Missy entered the living room to find Richard standing in front of the family portrait which hung over the fireplace. "This is Missy Calhoun," Becky introduced her friend.

Missy reached out her hand.

Richard shook her hand. "I'm so sorry for your loss. Your parent's lawyer, Rodney Sims, sends his apologies. He's home sick and forgot to send me before now to pick up the insurance policies and any other information you may have regarding their estate. I'll be working with him by phone since he is unable to come to the office. I assure you, I'll do everything possible to make details of the estate progress smoothly. Did you find the insurance policies?"

"Yes, I have them. Along with checking account information, and a few things I wasn't expecting to find." Missy turned to Becky. "Would you get the policies?" She looked back at Richard. "Is there anything else you might need now?"

"No," he said. "The life insurance policies will do for now. I'll need information regarding investments, but not immediately."

"We only found entries in the checkbook for American Funds, but we haven't completely gone through the file cabinet. What will you need concerning the investments?"

"I'll need any documentation which shows the account numbers and any beneficiaries. Sometimes the forms are hard to understand. Mr. Sims will review the documents and transfer the investments into your name."

Becky returned to the living room and handed the files to Richard. "Could you excuse us just a minute?" She took Missy by the hand and guided her into the hallway. "Do you think the lawyer will need these?" Becky gave her the adoption papers.

"I don't know, but I guess this may complicate matters." Missy went back into the living room where Richard stood reviewing the policies. "Earlier I said we found something unexpected." Missy handed the envelope to him and then sat down. "I think it may be important."

Richard looked at the papers and then at Missy. "You didn't know you were adopted?"

Missy frowned as she shook her head.

"I found those in the file cabinet while looking for the investment files," Becky explained. "Does this cause a problem with the estate?"

"No, even with this information," Richard said while indicating the envelope in his hand. "You are the beneficiary. If I may, I'd like to take the adoption papers and copy them for our files. I'll bring the originals back to you. Okay?"

"Yes," Missy replied.

"Excuse me," Cissy said from the door.

Richard looked up at Cissy; a look of surprise spread over his face.

Missy stood. "Let me introduce you. This is Richard Jameson, one of my lawyers, and Richard, this is my twin sister, Cissy."

"Hello . . ." Looking between the sisters, he said, "I didn't think you had any surviving relatives."

"That's what I thought too, until today. You see, Cissy came here after meeting with Becky. It's a long story, but as it turns out, I have four sisters who I didn't remember."

"I saw her on the news." Cissy indicated her twin. "We knew right away that she's our long-lost sister."

"This is something Mr. Sims needs to know right away." Richard glanced between them.

"This won't be a problem will it?" Becky asked.

"No, it shouldn't be, but it adds a whole new aspect to the case." Richard shook his head. "I . . . we may have to get more details on the adoption. If there aren't any in here." He held up the envelope with the adoption papers.

"You can see for yourself, we're twin sisters." Cissy stepped beside her twin. "If you'll come with me, I'll introduce you to the rest of our family, and you'll know we're related." Cissy looked upset and took him by the arm leading him down the hallway toward the family room before Missy and Becky could stop her.

"Dottie, Joy, Gayle, this is Missy's lawyer. I feel he doesn't believe we're her sisters." Cissy looked right at Richard with eyes blazing.

Richard held up his hands. "I didn't say I didn't believe you. It's just, well, you came into Missy's life at a time when she's a very easy target. I only want to protect her."

"I know they're my sisters." Missy entered the room with Becky behind her. "They aren't trying to scam me. Look at us. Tell me we're not related."

Missy and her four sisters stood side by side.

"I see what you mean." Richard nodded. "Please accept my apologies." He waved his hand toward them. "I guess I wasn't expecting anything like this."

"I'm Dottie Walker, the oldest. I'm also a lawyer." She stepped forward and gave him her card. "You can look me up on the Texas Bar Association. My husband, Travis, is also a lawyer. I assure you this is all above board. We were separated when the twins were three and were never allowed to know what happened to them. It's only by God's grace I found Cissy about a year ago. We've been looking for Missy all this time."

"You know I must protect my client at all cost. This is so unusual, ah, I'm sorry. I do believe you," Richard replied as he turned to Missy. "I think I have what Mr. Sims needs and will be leaving now. I'll let you know if he needs anything else." He nodded to each of them. "Ladies, good day." Then walked down the hallway to the front door.

Cissy followed him. "I'm glad you believe us. Missy is our sister and it is so good to feel whole again. We'll be with her tomorrow at the funerals. Will you be there?"

"I'm not sure, as I've never met Missy before today. I'll see what Mr. Sims wants me to do, but I will see you again. I am sure of it." Richard opened the door and walked out.

Cissy walked back to the family room and stood in the doorway for several minutes.

Missy broke her twin's train of thought. "Cissy, could you stay here with me and Becky tonight?"

Cissy grinned and nodded, too choked up to say anything for a few seconds. "I would love to, Missy. I'll have to go home and get some things and tell my parents what's happened since this morning. I'll come back and be with you tonight and tomorrow. Now that we've found you, we're not letting you out of our sight."

"No, we're here to stay in your life if you'll let

us." Gayle smiled.

"We've waited so long to see you again, we aren't going away." Joy agreed.

Dottie touched Missy's arm. "If you need any help, we're here for you."

The sisters gathered their things to leave and assured Missy they would be at the funeral the next day. Each one hugged her again before leaving.

Becky walked them to the door. "I'm so glad this turned out as it did." She opened the front door. "Cissy, do you know when you'll be back? Missy needs to eat, and if you could be back for supper, it would be great."

"I'll be here around five and will bring dessert."

After Becky closed the door, she walked back to where Missy sat. "Are you okay?"

"I have four sisters. I'm getting an image in my head of Christmas and all of us sitting in front of the decorated tree, each with one gift. I can't remember what our mother looked like, but I can feel the love she had for all of us."

"I'm sure more memories will come back as you talk with your sisters. Would you please take a nap now?"

"I'll try but no promises. I want to be up when Cissy returns. Can you believe it? I have a family even when I thought I'd lost all of mine." Tears came to her eyes and she didn't stop them from falling this time. "I don't know if these are tears of sorrow or joy. I remember the verse stating God would give me a peace which passes all understanding, and He's given me more than I expected." Missy rose and went upstairs to rest. Soon her eyes closed, and she slept soundly for the first time since the accident.

Chapter 4

Missy woke to the smell of garlic. She looked at the clock. *It's already six. No wonder my stomach's growling.* Still a little groggy, she got up and wondered if she'd dreamed everything. *Could Momma be downstairs fixing dinner?* She ran downstairs to the kitchen but came to an abrupt stop when she saw Becky at the stove. "I guess I was dreaming."

Becky turned to her. "You slept a few hours, so you may have dreamed. It wasn't the nightmare, was it?"

"No, it was . . ." Before Missy could finish, Cissy joined them.

"I thought I heard your voice. How do you feel?" Cissy asked.

"I thought I imagined you." Missy smiled. "But I see you're real."

Cissy nodded, walked to Missy and hugged her. "I'm very real. I put my stuff in your brother's room. Hope it's okay."

"Yes, of course." Missy smiled slightly.

"Are you hungry?" Becky indicated the pot on

the stove.

"You must've heard my stomach growl." Missy patted her belly. "Whatever you're cooking, it smells wonderful."

"Good. I made spaghetti and meatballs, garlic bread, and a salad. Cissy brought dessert."

"I don't know if I can eat a lot, but I am hungry." Missy rubbed her stomach. "What did you bring for dessert?"

Cissy smiled. "When we were little, your favorite dessert was lemon meringue pie. Is it still?"

"I love it. You remembered?"

"Yes, lots of things about us are surfacing. Do you recall anything yet?"

"I had an image of all of us sitting by a Christmas tree." Missy told her twin her vision. She frowned. "I guess we were about two or three years old."

"I can't remember Momma's face either." Cissy sighed. "But Dottie has a photograph of all of us, and it's just as you described. You must've seen the picture after it was taken."

"I don't know, but if I could see it, maybe more memories will come back."

"Everything is ready to eat if both of you will help me put it on the table." Becky gestured to the bowls of food.

Cissy picked up the salad bowl. Missy grabbed the basket of bread, and Becky followed them to the table with the pot of spaghetti and meatballs.

As they sat, Missy asked, "Cissy, would you

bless the meal Becky prepared?"

"Yes, certainly." Cissy extended her hands to Becky and Missy. "Lord, what an amazing God you are. You've protected Missy all these years and sent her Becky, a wonderful friend and sister in Christ. I thank you, dear Lord, for reuniting us with our sister after all this time. I pray the loss she's suffered will be eased some by having us by her side today, tomorrow, and the future. I lift Ryan to you dear Lord. You know where he is, and the urgency for him to be here. Please keep him in the safety of your hands and bring him home soon. Thank you, Lord, for this food before us and the hands which prepared it. In the name of Jesus Christ. Amen."

In unison, Becky and Missy echoed "Amen." They both looked at Cissy, squeezing each other's hands and smiled.

Peace filled Missy. *God is lovingly guiding my life and providing me with the strength and peace I need to face tomorrow and whatever the future holds. I feel a peace only God can give.*

They chatted as they ate as if being together was a normal everyday thing.

"I'm in my last year of college," Cissy told them. "I'll finish my degree in education and plan to be an elementary teacher. I love the kindergarten age best."

"I'm getting my degree in education, too," Missy uttered. "I want to teach drama in high school." She looked at her twin. "I can't believe how much our lives are alike."

"I wonder why our paths never crossed. Where are you going to college?"

"At Midwestern State University. Where are you going?"

"MSU, too, but taking night classes." Cissy declared. "I started working part-time at a daycare during the summer before college started and loved it. My boss offered me a full-time position and I accepted it to help pay for my college. Now, she's giving me a few hours a day off to do my student teaching."

"You two have a lot in common," Becky commented.

"Yes, and it's so strange." Missy smiled at her sister. "Living in the same town all these years and never seeing each other. I wonder how many people saw me and thought they saw you."

"You know, a couple of times people have stopped me and talked to me as if they knew me, but I didn't know them." Cissy smiled. "They must've been friends of yours."

"I wonder what they thought?" Missy chuckled.

"They probably thought I seemed strange but didn't know why."

After dinner, with dishes in the dishwasher and a clean kitchen, they retired to the family room to continue talking.

"We both went to a Christian school. Where did you go?" Becky asked.

"I went to Hirschi High School," Cissy replied. "It's a good school with lots of kids whose parents were stationed at Sheppard Air Force Base."

Missy grew quiet listening to her twin and friend talk.

Becky finally noticed Missy wasn't joining in on the conversation and asked, "Are you okay?"

"I guess I'm still trying to sort things out in my mind," Missy replied. "We have very similar backgrounds but, at the same time, very different. I'm still trying to remember when we were little, but besides the one image of Christmas, I don't remember anything else."

"It's understandable," Becky affirmed. "So much has happened, and you were so young."

Missy yawned, "I'm getting tired too and tomorrow will be a very long and hard day. Shall we call it a night?"

Becky and Cissy nodded in agreement, exchanging hugs, and went upstairs to their rooms.

Just before Missy entered her room, she turned back to Cissy. "Thank you for finding me."

Cissy hugged her again. "God brought us back together at a time when you needed us. I'll always be your sister and will be here when you need me. Remember, God promised to never leave you nor forsake you. I think our reunion is His way of showing you He loves you. I love you, too, Sis." Cissy held Missy for a long moment and then stepped back and noticed tears rolling down her checks. "Hey, I didn't mean to make you cry."

"These are tears of joy." Missy wiped her eyes.

"God knew how much I'd need someone with me, and He brought all of you to me. Now, if only Ryan would call."

Becky approached Missy and took her hands. "He'll be here as soon as he can, but it may not be tomorrow. I think he's on his way back to you; I feel it deep down in my heart." She gave Missy's hands a squeeze.

"I feel it, too." Missy reached out a hand to her twin. "Can we say a prayer for Ryan's safe travel and for me to have God's strength to get through tomorrow?"

Becky started the prayer. "Lord, we come to you with humble hearts asking you to put angels around Ryan and Missy. We've seen a miracle today in the reunion of the sisters and only you, Lord, could have done it. Please give her your peace which passes all understanding, tonight, tomorrow, and all the tomorrows to come." Becky squeezed Cissy's hand.

Cissy continued the prayer. "My awesome Jesus Christ, my Lord, and Savior. How great you are. Thank you, dear Lord, for bringing our family back together. Your timing for us to be here for my sister is perfect. Lord, we know Ryan is in your plan for Missy, and I pray he'll be here tomorrow to support her. Thank you, Lord, for such a wonderful friend Missy has in Becky; I pray I can become her friend also. I ask now, Lord, that you grant us all a good night's sleep. In Christ's precious name. Amen."

In unison, Becky and Missy echoed, "Amen."

"Thank you both for being here." Missy smiled

at her friend and sister.

As they separated to go to their rooms for the night, the phone rang. "Please answer the phone, Becky." Missy indicated the phone in her room.

"Hello, Calhoun residence."

"Hi, Becky. This is Ryan. Can I speak with Missy?"

"Yes, of course." Becky smiled while handing the phone to Missy without indicating who had called.

"Hello." Missy voice quivered.

"Missy, it's me, Ryan. Are you okay?"

"Ryan?" Missy's eyes filled with tears of relief. "Are you on your way home?" She looked at Becky and Cissy standing just outside her door.

"Yes, it took a few days for me to get the message. We were on patrol. I got on the next flight and I'm hoping to be with you tomorrow. Sorry, I haven't called before now, but my phone was damaged while we were on patrol. A very generous person sitting next to me heard my story and is letting me use his phone to call you."

"I'm so thankful you'll be here soon. Oh, Ryan, I have so much to tell you."

"Missy, I've got to go. The plane is about to land in New York. Love you. See you tomorrow. Bye."

"Love you, too. Looking forward to seeing you. Bye." Missy hung up the phone, turned and smiled at Becky and Cissy. "He's coming home. He'll be here sometime tomorrow."

"Oh, I'm so happy for you Missy," Becky

exclaimed coming into the room. She reached out to hug her.

"Me too." Cissy joined in the hug.

"I'm so happy," Missy announced. "Now, I think I can sleep. I'll have his voice in my ears to help me."

Becky and Cissy left the room saying a final "goodnight."

Finally, alone, Missy prepared for bed. She giggled when she saw her reflection in the mirror. She couldn't help but smile thinking of being with Ryan the next day.

Chapter 5

The next morning, Ryan's cab stopped in front of Missy's house. He ran to the front door, rang the bell, and prepared to wrap his arms around his Missy.

Mrs. Stevens answered the door.

"Hello, Mrs. Stevens. I guess I missed her." Ryan sighed.

"You'd better hurry, she left about thirty minutes ago headed for the church."

Ryan looked toward the street, but his cab had already left. He turned back to Mrs. Stevens. "Can I leave my duffle bag here? If I want to make it, I'll have to run, and I can't with this."

Mrs. Stevens shook her head as she reached for the duffle bag. "You can't run all the way to the church." She pulled her car keys out of her pocket and handed them to Ryan. "Here, you can drive my car. I'm not going anyplace. I'm the house sitter until the funerals are over and Missy returns."

Ryan leaned over and kissed her cheek. "Thanks. You always know just what is needed for others. I'll bring it right back after the funerals."

* * *

It took a few minutes for Ryan to find a parking space at the church. He walked toward the building looking at all the cars. *It's sad it had to be a funeral to bring all these people together.*

He entered the church as the service started and took long strides down the aisle toward the front where Missy sat. He saw Missy with her head down. Becky sat on one side and another lady on the other side. He did a double take at the other lady, shook his head, and mumbled to himself, "She looks just like Missy."

Becky noticed Ryan and stood up. She let him take her place.

Missy looked up and gasped. She reached for Ryan, pulling him down to sit beside her. She hugged him tightly and whispered in his ear, "I knew you'd be here. We prayed for God to bring you home safely."

"I felt His presence during my trip," Ryan replied. He pulled back and looked into her eyes as he wiped the tears from her cheek. "I love you."

Missy smiled at Ryan. "I love you, too. So much has happened and I have a lot to tell you." She nodded toward her sisters sitting in the pew.

Ryan looked at each of them and his gaze stopped at Cissy. He started to say something when the singer started her song.

Missy whispered, "Later. There's too much to tell right now."

Ryan nodded and kept glancing from Missy to Cissy. Then he turned his attention toward the front of the sanctuary and held Missy's hand through the service.

When the eulogy ended, Ryan helped Missy to walk to each of the three caskets to say goodbye to her parents and brother.

Missy trembled, and tears rolled down her face. She nearly collapsed when reaching her mother's casket. Ryan held her around the waist for support. She tried to be strong, but the grief showed on her face as she went from one casket to the other saying, "I love you so very much and I miss you."

When Ryan knew Missy said her final goodbye, he escorted her down the aisle, out the door, and over to the cemetery next to the church. Ryan sat with Missy under the awning, turned, and looked her full in the face. "Missy, you are so dear to me. I can't imagine what you're going through. But I'm here now to help you."

Tears fell but Missy managed a nod. "I know and I'm so very glad."

The graveside service was short. White doves were released, and they circled the cemetery several times before flying off. Everyone stopped by and spoke to Missy.

Pastor Kevin waited until last to offer his condolences. "Missy, if I can do anything for you, just give me a call."

Missy reached for his hand. "Thank you for the

service. It was more of a celebration of life rather than a funeral."

The pastor smiled. "It's what your dad told me he wanted whenever his time came. I just did it for all of them. Remember, call me if you need any help or need to talk. Okay?"

"Thank you, Pastor." Missy watched him leave then turned to Ryan. "Do you believe in miracles?"

"Yes, you're my miracle," Ryan replied.

Missy smiled and pointed to her sisters who stood nearby. "Well, they're my miracles."

Missy could see by his facial expressions, he didn't understand. "Ryan, I have four sisters."

Ryan's mouth opened, but nothing came out. He took a deep breath and frowned. "I don't understand."

"Let's go back to the house, and I'll explain everything." She turned to her sisters. "I want all of you to come with us to the house."

"We would love to, but are you sure?" Cissy asked.

Missy nodded.

They walked to the limousine waiting to take them back to Missy's home.

Ryan opened the door then paused. "Wait! I drove Mrs. Steven's car. I have to take it back to the house."

Becky held out her hand. "Give me the keys, I'll drive it back." She turned to the sisters, and asked, "Would any of you girls like to ride with me?"

"I will." Came the reply from all of them.

Missy mouthed, "Thank you." Then entered the limousine.

The quick drive back to the house wasn't time to answer the millions of questions they both had, so they spent it wrapped in an embrace, with lots of kissing. Ryan kept whispering softly in her ear "I love you and missed you so much."

Missy's heart was full of joy with his loving embrace. She snuggled deeper into his arms and sighed with contentment.

* * *

Mrs. Stevens had sandwiches with all the trimmings prepared for them when they returned.

"Thank you so very much, Mrs. Stevens." Missy smiled. "I'm grateful for what you've done for me."

"Missy, you've been one of my girls since I taught you in third grade. I'll do everything I can to make this time of loss easier for you."

Becky arrived at the house right after Missy. She handed the keys to Mrs. Stevens and hugged her. "Thanks for letting Ryan use your car to get to the church. He arrived just in time."

Mrs. Stevens nodded with a tear in her eye, and then left the house.

"Anyone hungry?" Becky asked. "Missy take Ryan to the family room and I'll bring you both a plate. We'll give you some time to explain to Ryan what's going on."

"Thank you, Becky." Missy took Ryan's hand and led him to the back of the house. They sat on the couch together. Ryan leaned in for a kiss. "I can't get enough kisses. I've been dreaming of you every night."

"The time we've been apart was agonizing," Missy said and then kissed Ryan again. "I can't believe you're here."

They were kissing when Becky entered the room. She cleared her throat. "Sorry for the interruption. Here are your sandwiches, although I don't think eating is on your minds right now. I'll set them here for you." She left the plates on the coffee table in front of the couch and headed back to the kitchen.

Ryan smiled. "Do you know what a great friend you have in Becky?"

"Yes, I do. She came yesterday and interceded for me with the reporters, helped me find the life insurance policies and . . . and Ryan, I must tell you what else Becky found in Daddy's file."

"Does it have to do with your sisters?" Ryan asked.

"Yes." Missy swallowed and took a deep breath. "Ryan, I'm adopted."

"Wow. You didn't know?"

"No, it came as a complete surprise. I don't know why they didn't tell me. I've so many questions, but the people who can answer them are gone." Tears rolled down her face. "I am so confused with everything. I really haven't processed the fact of being adopted and everything missing from my memory . . . my sisters, my mother, and father . . . who I am . . ."

"Missy, you know who you are, the love of my life. You've had so much happen this past week. You may have a whole new family, but you are still the lovely girl I fell in love with. You're the only one who can make me laugh at myself when I do stupid things. You always see me as me, not what I wanted others to see. The Missy I love is right here in my arms. The fact of your adoption won't change anything. I know you, my love." He hugged her tight and kissed her again. "You still want to marry me in four months, don't you?"

Missy's face brightened. "The thought of marrying you gave me hope in the days after the accident. It kept me going. But yesterday when the adoptions papers were found, I thought maybe you wouldn't want to marry me and . . ."

Ryan stopped her words with a kiss. "How could you question the way I feel for you? You're not any different today than when you said yes to my marriage proposal. I know a lot has changed, but you haven't, I haven't, nor has my love for you. Missy, you're my soul mate."

Missy snuggled closer. "Kiss me again, so I know all of this isn't a dream."

He did and then held her in silence. Finally, Ryan turned to Missy. "Now, what is this about you having four sisters, and why does one of them look exactly like you? I thought I was seeing double."

Missy laughed and grabbed Ryan's hands. "Let's

go see my sisters and they'll help explain everything."

They found her sisters and Becky eating at the dining room table.

Becky stood. "Is everything okay?"

"Yes, I just thought it was time for Ryan to really meet my sisters and let them explain everything to him." Missy smiled.

"Here, sit down." Becky motioned to two chairs. "I'll go get your plates, which I'm sure you haven't touched. What do you want to drink? Water, iced tea, or soda?"

"I'd like some iced tea," Ryan replied. "Thanks."

"I'd like the same, please," Missy answered.

Becky left to get their food.

Missy took the seat next to Cissy and put her arm around her and looked at Ryan. "Ryan, I'd like you to meet Cissy, my twin sister."

"Cissy, a twin, that explains it. My mind couldn't wrap around seeing her. It's amazing, simply amazing." Ryan grinned at Cissy as he offered his hand.

Cissy stood, moved to Ryan, and hugged him. "So, you'll be my brother-in-law. It's great to meet you."

Becky returned to the dining room and set their plates and drinks in front of the couple. Then she sat on the other side of Cissy.

Missy introduced the other sisters. They too, hugged Ryan. "Dottie knows the whole story, and how we became separated." She turned to Dottie. "Would you tell Ryan what happened?"

"I would love to tell him the story since it now

has a happy ending," Dottie looked at Ryan. "Go ahead and eat, it's a long story."

Dottie gave Ryan the details and answered all his questions.

Missy absorbed the information with a clearer head.

The doorbell rang, and Becky jumped up. "I'll get it." When she returned, Richard Jameson followed. "Mr. Jameson asked to come in to talk with you, Missy." She picked up her plate and drink and motioned for him to sit in the vacated chair next to Cissy.

Missy looked alarmed. "Is anything wrong with the papers I gave you?"

"No, no, everything's fine. I just wanted to return these documents to you and tell you it was a beautiful service." Richard handed the envelope to Missy. "Mr. Sims already had a copy of the adoption papers. He knew about it and said he frequently suggested to your parents to tell you, but they wouldn't listen to him."

"He knew all the time?" Missy frowned. "Did he say why my parents didn't want to tell me?"

"No, he didn't say anything else. I'm sorry, it's all I know." Richard shrugged. "When Mr. Sims is well and back in the office you can talk with him." He kept glancing over at Cissy.

Missy nodded. "I will. Can you let me know when he's back at the office?"

"Yes." Richard stood. "Well, if there's nothing else, I'll go now, so I don't intrude anymore." He looked at Missy and nodded at Cissy.

"Richard, wait, please join us." Missy smiled. "Dottie just told Ryan, my fiancé, our story, and we were just talking about it. Can I fix you a sandwich, or perhaps Cissy can show you what we have in the kitchen?"

Cissy stood. "Yes, please stay."

"I would like to get to know you." Richard looked at Cissy then back at Missy. "All of you better. Thanks."

"It's just sandwiches, potato salad, and chips. Come this way." Cissy took Richard's hand and led him toward the kitchen, stopped, turned, and asked, "Can I get anyone anything?"

"No, I think we're fine," Missy replied with a soft laugh.

Cissy looked at her twin and asked, "What?"

Missy just smiled, shook her head, and waved her away.

After they were out of ear shot, Missy whispered, "Am I the only one picking up on the electricity between these two?"

A resounding "no" came from the others.

"I saw the sparks flying yesterday when they met," Becky commented. "While you slept yesterday afternoon, Cissy kept asking questions about him, which I couldn't answer because I'd just met him, too."

"This is the first time I've seen Cissy interested in a guy." Dottie grinned. "Do you want me to check him out?"

Missy shook her head. "Since he works for my

parents' law firm, I'll ask Mr. Sims about him." Her thoughts turned to her parents and brother. Tears formed in her eyes and she blinked them away.

Cissy and Richard returned to the dining room and everyone could see the twinkle in their eyes and grins on each face.

Missy smiled and whispered to Ryan, "Yes, there is something going on between those two."

Ryan nodded in agreement, took Missy's hand and squeezed it. "It's nothing compared to us."

* * *

After they finished eating, Becky began picking up plates. "Let's go to the family room. I'll make coffee, and we can have dessert."

"Sounds good to me." Cissy replied as she picked up glasses.

The other sisters gathered the remaining dishes and followed Becky to the kitchen.

"Just leave everything in the sink until later." Missy took Ryan's hand and led him into the family room. The others followed.

"Do you remember the day Cissy tried to climb up on the counter to get the cookies while we were doing laundry?" Joy asked her sisters.

Dottie nodded. "She achieved her goal but getting down, the chair tipped over while she stood on the back."

Gayle giggled. "I never saw her so scared when

we rushed in and saw her hanging on the cabinet door."

"Where was I?" Missy asked.

"You were standing by the toppled chair holding the bag of cookies," Joy explained.

"You always went along with Cissy in her antics which got you both in trouble."

"Did she get hurt?" Missy looked at her twin.

"No," Dottie replied. "We got there just in time to keep her from falling."

Cissy snickered. "I guess I wanted a cookie."

They all laughed.

Missy felt grateful that Ryan was there to hear everything.

Ryan asked about Gayle's fiancé and learned his squadron was stationed at the same base. "I'll try to see him when I get back." *How am I going to tell Missy, I must return soon?*

* * *

Later that afternoon, the doorbell sounded, and Becky went to answer it. She returned with some ladies from the church. "They brought more food," she told the group in the family room.

Missy stood and went to the ladies. "Thank you so much. I hadn't even thought about what we would eat for dinner."

Mrs. Stevens smiled. "I didn't think you would and wanted to make sure you had something hot to eat. I brought you chicken enchiladas, Lily brought the rice and beans, and Margie fixed chocolate cake."

"It all sounds wonderful. Let's put it in the kitchen." Missy led the way. "Y'all are very special doing this for me."

"It's our pleasure." Mrs. Stevens placed the casserole in the oven and set it to low. "It's still hot but this will keep it warm until you decide to eat."

Missy gave each lady a kiss on the cheek and a hug. "I'm blessed to have each of you in my life. Thank you so much."

"We're sorry for your loss." Lily patted Missy on her arm.

"Your parents were dear friends, and I'll miss them so much." Margie wiped a tear from her cheek.

Tears formed in Missy's eyes. "You've made this day better by your generosity."

"We'll leave you to your company. I can bring more food tomorrow if you want, just call me." Mrs. Stevens hugged her.

Missy walked them to the front door and watched them as they went to their car. She didn't see any reporters, but the patrol car and black truck were still at the curb. She shook her head and went back to join her sisters and friends.

Dottie, Joy, and Gayle were gathering their things.

"You're not leaving, are you?" Missy asked her sisters.

"Yes, I need to get home to let the babysitter

go," Joy replied.

"It's been a good afternoon getting to know you better." Gayle picked up her purse.

"Let me know if you need help with anything." Dottie took Missy's hand. "It seems Richard has the estate process in control, but I'll help if you want me to."

"I have full confidence in Mr. Sims, so I'm sure Richard is following his instructions." Missy squeezed her sister's hand. "You have helped me so much already. Thank you."

The three sisters left after making plans for a sleepover. The date depended on Joy's husband's schedule, so he could take care of their little boy.

* * *

The others talked more and ate the meal the ladies brought. But soon the day turned into night.

Missy, Ryan, and Becky stood at the front door and watched as Richard walked Cissy to her car. He carried her overnight bag and stood talking for a while before she got in and drove off. Then he left too.

Missy looked at Becky and Ryan. "There's definitely something going on between them. I like Richard, don't you?"

Both agreed and then they went back into the house.

As Becky reached the kitchen, she turned to Ryan and Missy. "I'll tidy the kitchen then head upstairs to bed. I'm sure y'all have plenty to talk about. Goodnight."

Missy and Ryan went into the family room and sat on the couch.

"Ryan, did you call your parents when you arrived?"

"No, but I called them from the airport, and I saw them at the funeral. I didn't get a chance to talk to them. They know I'm needed here with you today. They do expect me home sometime tonight but right now, we need to talk."

Missy's eyes widened. "Is something wrong? The stories tonight didn't make you change your mind, did they?"

"No, Missy." Ryan kissed her hand. "We'll be married when I return home, but I need to go back on Sunday."

"You can't stay longer?" Missy's eyes pooled with tears.

"No. My commander gave approval for a week here in the states. I know it's not much time to be together, but we can savor each minute." Ryan touched his lips to her forehead, her cheek, and finally her lips. A lingering, sweet kiss. He held Missy in his arms. "I love you so very much, and I'm sorry I have to go back so soon."

"I knew you'd have to go back, but I thought we'd have more time." Missy smiled trying to be brave. *Will the loneliness return when he and Becky leave? Will my sisters still be around?* She wasn't sure, but she knew her life wouldn't be the same. She would have to fully rely on God to adjust.

Ryan held Missy close and whispered, "While I'm away, remember, I love you and can't wait until you're my wife."

Missy smiled and returned his kiss. "I love you too. I'm counting the days. There is so much to do for the wedding, and I don't know what to do next."

"Don't worry about it. I want you to have a good night's sleep." Ryan hugged her. "Now I must go and get some rest. I haven't slept much since I heard the news and couldn't on the plane. I'm exhausted. Remember, you're the love of my life." He stood and pulled Missy up into his arms for another a goodnight kiss.

They walked arm-in-arm down the hallway to the front door.

"Dream about us tonight, Missy." Ryan held her tight. "Tomorrow we'll pick up where we left off." He kissed her again, grabbed his duffle bag, opened the door, and stepped out.

Saying goodnight to Ryan left Missy feeling the sadness of the day. She put on a brave smile and waved to him as he walked down the street toward his parent's home.

Chapter 6

The next morning, Missy woke with a smile on her face. A whole night's sleep without a nightmare, a welcome change. Lingering remnants of the dream she did have flitted through her mind. She saw herself in a gorgeous gown ready to walk down the aisle. All her sisters and Becky stood at the front of the church waiting for her. Ryan stood in his dress uniform with the groomsmen beside him. *Breathtaking. It's how I want my wedding to be.* She took a deep breath to slow her rapidly beating heart while praying the real wedding would be just as beautiful.

Missy showered and dressed. The smell of bacon cooking told her Becky was busy in the kitchen making sure she had food to eat. Going downstairs, an image of Ryan flashed before her eyes. His handsome face, gentle smile, and sparkling blue eyes framed by dark brown hair as he went down on one knee to propose marriage to her. She turned the corner into the kitchen. "Becky, whatever you're . . ." Her sentence hung in mid-air. It wasn't Becky cooking; it was Ryan.

He looked up. "Well, good morning, beautiful.

You look like you slept well." He walked over and kissed her with a spatula in one hand and a dish towel over his shoulder.

"Good morning, handsome. You'll make a good-looking house husband to some lucky girl. Do you have anyone in mind for a wife?" Missy smiled shyly.

"Yep, she's a pretty little thing with shiny blonde hair and blue eyes like the Texas sky."

"Does this woman have a name?"

"Well, of course she has a name, but it'll be a better name when she'll be called Mrs. Ryan Franklin." Ryan hugged Missy and gave her a quick kiss.

Missy giggled and hugged him back. "Hey, I think something's burning."

"Oh, no." Ryan quickly returned to the stove to flip a pancake. "It's okay, at least it doesn't have sand in it."

"Sand?" Missy asked.

"Most of the food we eat overseas seems to get sand in it. The only food without sand is from the mess hall when we're on base, which isn't often."

"Good morning, Missy," Becky greeted her friend as she entered the kitchen from the dining room.

"Good morning. I see Ryan put you to work." Missy smiled.

Becky nodded.

"These pancakes are ready. Becky, do you have the table set?"

"Yes, slave driver." Becky winked at Missy. "It's set to your specification. Do you want me to pour the juice and bring out the hot tea?"

"Yes, please." Ryan put the last of the pancakes on a plate, picked it up, along with a plate of bacon to take to the dining room.

"What can I do to help?" Missy asked.

"Not a thing, my love. Today, you're going to be pampered. I've taken care of everything." Ryan grinned as he entered the dining room.

Missy followed thinking how she loved his mischievous grin. "Okay, but I expect to learn the details of what you two have cooked up for me, and I don't mean this wonderful breakfast." Missy sat and picked up her napkin and placed it on her lap.

"It's all Ryan's doing. I know nothing." Becky set the juice and tea on the table.

"You'll both find out soon enough. Now, let's eat this breakfast I've slaved over." Ryan placed the plates of pancakes and bacon in front of Missy.

"Yes, sir." Missy saluted Ryan and then laughed as the others joined her. "The table is beautiful, Becky. I love the fresh flowers; daffodils are my favorite."

"Ryan brought the flowers. I just added the napkins, plates, and silverware," Becky replied.

Ryan smiled. "I'll say the blessing. Dear Lord, thank you for this day and the meal You have provided. I'm praying this day will be a blessing to all of us. Bless this food to the nourishment of our bodies. In Jesus Christ's name. Amen."

"Thanks, Ryan." Missy put a pancake on her plate. She added butter and syrup, took a bite, and sighed. "Ryan, these are really good. I like the pecans in them. I've never had pancakes like this."

"My Mom always puts pecans in the batter. It's a favorite of mine."

"Good to know because when we're married, I'll make pancakes like this for you." As Missy ate, she saw the glances between Ryan and Becky. She took her last bite of pancake and set her fork on her plate. "Okay, spill it."

Both looked at her and then at each other. Ryan gave her a mischievous grin. "Spill what?"

"The reason you and Becky keep looking at each other like kids with a secret. Let me in on it."

"Well, I do have a surprise for you." Ryan grinned.

"What is it?" Missy anxiously asked while dabbing her lips with her napkin.

"You'll have to wait a few more minutes . . ." The doorbell rang, cutting off Ryan in mid-sentence.

Becky jumped up. "I'll get it." She sprinted to the door and soon returned with Cissy following.

"Ryan, I got here as soon as I could after you called. What's going on?" Cissy asked.

"That's what I want to know." Missy crossed her arms over her chest and looked at Ryan.

"Okay, I'll tell you now. I've been waiting for Cissy to get here because she's part of the surprise."

"I am?" Cissy asked. She looked puzzled while she sat in the chair beside her sister.

"Yes, you and Becky, both are," Ryan answered

as he turned to his fiancée. "I've planned the day for you, Missy." He held up his hand to stop her from interrupting. "Last night, you told me you wanted to spend every minute with me while I'm here, but I think right now, you need something else, and I hope you'll agree." He took a deep breath and continued. "I've made reservations for you, Becky, Cissy, and your other three sisters to spend the day at the new spa which just opened."

"But, Ryan, you have to leave Sunday, and I want to be with you." Missy reached out and took Ryan's hand.

Ryan took hold of both her hands. "Sweetheart, you've been through some very traumatic days, but the last couple days had a mix of happiness. You need time to spend with your sisters to get to know them."

"I will, but I want to be with you while you're here," Missy pleaded.

"I know you do but listen." Ryan squeezed her hand. "I don't want to leave you as things stand now. You need to be completely comfortable with thinking of yourself as having sisters and not being alone. From what I heard last night, they truly love you and have missed you dearly." Ryan glanced at Cissy.

"Yes, I've missed you." Cissy smiled at Missy.

"Over the next few months while I'm gone, you'll need to rely on your sisters. Will you call them if you need help?" Ryan asked while he shook his head. "I don't think so. You won't call because you don't know them well enough and don't want to be a bother."

Missy lowered her eyes to their entwined hands and looked into Ryan's eyes. "You know me too well. I don't want to be a burden on anyone."

"You won't be a burden." Cissy leaned over and put a hand on Missy's shoulder. "We want to be a part of your life. We've already missed so much of it."

Missy's eyes filled with tears and touched her twin's hand. "It's going to take time for me to adjust. It makes me feel good knowing you'll be here for me in the months to come."

Cissy caressed her sister's shoulder with tears in her eyes.

"Today starts a new journey of your life." Ryan kissed Missy's hands. "You'll need to know they'll be at your side, right along with me. They're a part of your family, a family that loves you, and thanks God for bringing you back to them. I'm going to have to rely on them to take care of you while I'm gone. I'll feel better if you and your sisters feel more comfortable together." He looked at Cissy and Becky. "Becky has always been like a sister to you and with her there, I hope you'll be more at ease. She wants to have time with you, too, before she has to leave."

"Yes, Missy, I wish I could stay longer but I can't because of my classes," Becky proclaimed.

"I've arranged for Dottie, Joy, and Gayle to meet the three of you at the spa," Ryan continued. "I've told the spa staff this is a family reunion: sisters' day. You get the works. Facials, manicures, pedicures, massages, and a new hair style if you want. I'm picking up the tab and whatever my future bride wants, she'll have it. Any questions?"

All three ladies looked at each other, grinning, and shook their heads in agreement. They stood and surrounded Ryan in a group hug.

After a few moments, Cissy and Becky stepped back.

"Ryan, how did I get so lucky to have you in my life?" Missy asked as she kissed and hugged him again. Tears streamed down her face.

Ryan kissed the tip of her nose. "Isn't God wonderful? I knew the moment I saw you, God sent you into my life. You're my soul mate, an answer to my prayers."

Ryan and Missy kissed again, oblivious of the other two in the room.

"Ahem," Becky uttered. "When are we supposed to be at the spa?"

Ryan glanced at his watch. "The appointment is in half an hour."

"What? I can't be ready by then!" Missy started out of the room, stopped, and turned back to Ryan. "I guess I can, since everything I'd do to go out, will be redone when we get to the spa, right?"

Ryan laughed. "Yes, sweetheart. The staff at the spa will be more interested in how you look when you leave. Either way, you're beautiful." Ryan stepped closer to Missy and kissed her. He looked at Cissy and Becky. "By the way, please plan to have dinner with Missy and me. I'm preparing a feast, with a little help from Mom, as a celebration of your reunion. I've already talked to the others. They can't make it. Will you two come?"

Cissy glanced at Becky then back at Ryan and Missy. "Ryan, don't you and Missy want to have some time alone?"

"We will, but tonight is Becky's last night here, and I'm sure Missy wants to spend it with her. I've already planned this with Becky, and she wants you here too, Cissy."

"Sure, Ryan. I'll need to call my parents and let them know what's going on. They thought something was wrong when you called so early this morning. I'll call them now." Cissy left the room.

"How can I thank you for this, Ryan?" Missy looked lovingly into his blue eyes.

"I want you to be happy, sweetheart. This is for me as much as it is for you. Just say, it's for my peace of mind while I'm gone. Okay?"

"Okay." She smiled. "Have I told you I love you today?"

Ryan shook his head. "Not until now. I love hearing it come from your lips." He kissed her and embraced her until he heard Cissy return.

"Everything is A-Okay with my parents." Cissy put her cell phone in her pocket. "I told them about your surprise and all they could say was 'Does he have a brother? You couldn't go wrong with someone like him.' Sorry, Ryan, my parents have been trying to match me up with someone. I think they want me to get on with my life, so they can travel more. I didn't mean it the way it sounded. They love me, and I know it, but I think they'd like to see me married and give them grandchildren. I keep telling them God just hasn't sent me the right guy yet, and until He does, no marriage or grandkids."

"Cissy, there's someone out there for you." Ryan smiled. "God will reveal him to you when the time is right." He winked at Missy. "Now, you three need to get moving. I have a kitchen to clean before Mom and Dad get here to help me prepare for dinner." Ryan took Missy by the shoulders and turned her toward Cissy and Becky. "She's in your hands now, keep her safe. Bring her back to me refreshed, relaxed, and smiling. The smile which makes my heart leap for joy." He bent down and kissed Missy on the cheek and whispered, "Don't worry about me. I intend to spend the day with my parents since I don't think I'll have much time the rest of the week. I plan on being with you every minute I can."

Chapter 7

They arrived at the spa to find Missy's siblings waiting for them. *They're my sisters. They're my sisters.* She kept repeating it over and over to herself, so she could believe what God was doing in her life.

"Hello," Missy greeted them. "I'm so glad y'all could be here."

"It's quite a treat. I'm lucky I didn't have to work today," Dottie stated. "You have a wonderful young man in Ryan. I was amazed when he told me he wanted to give us this spa day, so we could get to know each other better."

"He is wonderful." Missy sighed. "This will give us time to talk more about what we were like when we were all together. I want to hear more about all of you."

Everyone laughed and giggled throughout the day over little things. Ryan was right; Missy needed this time with her sisters. She started to relax around them, especially Cissy. *Being together feels natural, not strange. I feel a bond and occasionally, get a vision of something, but I'm not sure if it's a memory or not. Missy* saw a vision of Dottie reading a book to her and Cissy.

"Dottie, did you read to us?" Missy asked while they were having their mani/pedi.

Dottie nodded. "Yes, I read to you and Cissy every night at bedtime."

"I didn't know if the memory was real or imagined," Missy mused.

"Don't worry." Dottie smiled. "Memories may come back. Y'all were so young. Don't try to force remembering. Just give it time."

* * *

During the massage, Missy could feel the tension slowly slipping out of her body.

"Ah, this feels so good." Missy smiled as the masseuse rubbed her shoulders.

"You have quite a few knots, and I'm going to work them out." Norma, the masseuse, kept adding oil and rubbing Missy's shoulders and back.

"I didn't know I was so tense, but I've had a lot of stress in my life this past week."

"You sure have." Cissy agreed from the massage table next to her twin.

Norma placed heated rocks along Missy's spine. "I hope this helps relax you."

"It feels so good." Missy sighed.

"What do you do at home to help relieve your stress?" Norma asked.

"Reading my Bible is the biggest stress reliever

for me, but I've not been able to lately."

"Why not?" Norma asked while rubbing Missy's legs and feet.

"My family were killed in a car accident last week." Missy shuddered.

Norma stopped rubbing. "Oh, I'm so sorry for your loss. Now I know why you're so tense." She placed more rocks on Missy's back. "You were on TV, weren't you?"

"Yes, and it ended up being a mixed blessing."

"How?" Norma resumed the massage.

"I can answer that question," Cissy stated. "By her being on the news, I was able to find her."

"What do you mean find her? She's your twin, right?" Norma asked.

"Yes, but we were separated when we were three years old. Adopted by two different families after our mother died and haven't seen each other since." Missy replied.

"It turned out to be a blessing from God to reunite our family," Cissy said smiling. "This massage is something I needed, too."

"Another blessing from God gifted through Ryan." Missy smiled at the thought of the love of her life.

* * *

After the massages, the spa staff led them to their facials, and finally their hair stylists. All too soon, it was time to leave.

"I can't believe we've been here most of the day, but it's been great talking with all of you. I wish y'all could come to dinner tonight," Missy declared to her three older sisters.

"I wish we could, too," Gayle replied. "I already had plans to finalize some things for my wedding." She nodded at Dottie and Joy. "They're helping me."

"Oh, my gosh, it's coming up soon. I'm sure there are so many things to do. If I can help, tell me. I know I'm going to need help finishing my plans." Missy's eyes filled with tears. "My Mom was keeping track of the details. I'll have to find the book she kept so I'll know what's left to be done."

"We'll help in any way we can," Joy assured her.

"Yes, we'll help." Dottie caressed Missy's shoulder. "Just let us get Gayle's wedding over. I can't believe it's less than a month away."

"Missy, I want you to be a part of it." Gayle put her hand on her sister's arm. "The bridesmaid dresses are done, but I'm sure I can get another one made, if you want to be a bridesmaid."

"Oh, Gayle, I don't know what to say." Missy hugged her sister.

"Just say you'll be a part of my special day."

"But by adding me as a bridesmaid, you'll have to add a groomsman. Maybe there's something else I can do to be part of the wedding."

"You're right." Gayle shook her head. "Would you consider lighting the family candle?"

"Yes, I'd be honored." Missy grasped her sister's hand. "I want all of you in my wedding, also. I dreamed about it last night. Y'all were standing at the front of the church waiting for me to walk down the aisle. It'll make me very happy if each of you would be with me on my big day."

"Of course, we'd love to be part of it." Cissy clapped her hands. "Two sisters getting married, and we'll be at both as a family."

"A family is what I need right now," Missy whispered as tears started running down her face.

"Don't cry, you'll ruin your makeup." Cissy grabbed a tissue and started dabbing at Missy's face.

"I'm sorry." Missy took the tissue from her sister's hand and finished wiping away the tears.

"Don't say you're sorry." Becky put her arm around Missy's shoulder and gave her a squeeze. "You've every right to cry. I don't know how you're staying so strong considering everything that's happened."

"It's only by God's strength and the love of friends like you," Missy replied giving Becky a hug back. "Thanks for being with me." She turned to the others. "Thank you for your support and love. The accident turned my life upside down, but I can see God's hand is turning my grief into joy. Ryan's plan is working. I'm feeling more at ease around you and know I can ask for help if I need it while he's gone."

"Of course, you can ask for help, or even a listening ear." Dottie touched Missy's arm. "What can we do to repay Ryan for this day?"

"He is so generous, we need to do something." Joy agreed.

"I think he's wonderful, but I'm biased." Missy giggled. "I know all he wants in return, is for me to be happy and comfortable around y'all."

"You can rely on us." Cissy smiled. "But we'll have to come up with something to do for him when he gets back."

Everyone agreed.

"It's been a wonderful day, Missy," Gayle spoke for the sisters. "Tell Ryan thanks from all of us."

"I will." Missy smiled at her sisters. "Thank you for finding me."

Missy, Cissy, and Becky said goodbye to the others and drove back to Missy's house.

* * *

The aroma of fresh bread greeted them as they opened the door.

Missy led the way to the kitchen. "Yum, smells like Ryan's mom is making her wonderful baked chicken and fresh biscuits."

Ryan looked up from the stove and went to Missy. "Boy, what a sight to behold. You look wonderfully relaxed, and so beautiful. It's nice to see you without worry lines on your forehead." He kissed her lightly.

"Something smells good. Is your mother here?"

Cissy asked looking around. "I'd like to meet her."

"No, Mom and Dad left a while ago." Ryan declared. "Mom made sure everything was under control, and that I knew what to do, but I do have help. Hey, guys, where are you?"

The girls looked at Ryan and turned to see Richard Jameson and Becky's boyfriend, Daniel Parker, enter the kitchen.

Becky ran to Daniel and hugged him. "What are you doing here?"

"Ryan called me and asked if I could drive over for dinner. Aren't you happy to see me?"

"Of course, I am. It's just so unexpected." Becky turned to Ryan. "Thanks, Ryan." She introduced Cissy to Daniel.

"You look just like Missy," Daniel stated as they shook hands.

"Of course, we're twins." Cissy chuckled, then looked at Richard. "And what are you doing here?"

"Ryan invited me too." Richard smiled at her.

Missy noticed he hadn't taken his eyes off her twin since he entered the room.

"Well, everything's ready." Ryan picked up the hot pads. "I've kept everything warm while waiting on you ladies. Shall we?" He took the chicken and green bean casserole out of the oven. He handed hot pads to Daniel to take one of the hot dishes. "Richard, please take the salad and bread to the table."

The men led the way into the dining room as the ladies followed.

Everyone gathered around the table. Missy took Ryan's and Cissy's hands; the others did the same to form a circle. "Please, bless this meal, Ryan."

Ryan bowed his head. "Dear Lord, we've come together to share this meal. I pray for the people around this table. Thank you for their friendship. Thank you for this food. In Jesus Christ's name. Amen."

Ryan pulled out the chair for Missy as the other guys did the same for Becky and Cissy.

"This is wonderful, Ryan," Missy uttered after taking her first bite. "I love your mother's chicken. I'll need to thank her for all she's done for me." She took another bite. "Yum, so good."

"She was pleased to do it." Ryan picked up his fork. "Tell me about your day. Did it make a difference like I hoped it would?"

"Yes, everything transpired the way you wanted. A wonderful blessing." Missy took a sip of her iced tea. "We laughed, cried, and learned so much about each other better. Dottie told about some of Cissy's antics when we were little. From what my twin said, she still gets into situations without even knowing it." Missy glanced at her sister and smiled.

Cissy deep in discussion with Richard and didn't hear her name mentioned.

Missy grinned at Ryan and gestured toward them.

Ryan leaned in and whispered, "Richard is very interested in her. His nerves were showing waiting for y'all to return. I had to put him to work setting the table to give him something to do. I see God's hand in their meeting."

"I do, too." Missy took Ryan's hand. "God's been working so many miracles in my life lately. I'm glad to see some good things come out of what's happened. My life is going to be so different, and I pray I can be strong while you're gone. Maybe with my sisters around, the time will fly by, and you'll be back before I know it."

Ryan kissed her hand. "We'll get through the next few months and then we can start our life together. You'll have to keep me up on what's brewing between those two, okay?"

"Yes, I will." Missy looked around the table. Becky and Daniel had their heads together in conversation as well. *Will we remain good friends after I'm married?*

Discussion around the table varied. The guys talked sports, and wedding plans were the center of topic with the gals.

"I think it's time to clear the table and serve dessert." Ryan stood taking Missy's plate.

Richard and Daniel picked up the other plates and headed to the kitchen.

"Ryan is spoiling me." Missy looked at her friend and sister, as she dabbed her lips on her napkin. "I'm taking advantage of it while I can."

"I agree." Becky took a sip of tea.

"I like having someone wait on me." Cissy grinned.

"Here's dessert." Ryan placed a bowl of raspberry truffle ice cream before his fiancée.

Richard and Daniel brought in dessert bowls for the rest of them.

"One of my favorite ice creams." Missy savored the first bite.

"Of course, it is. Today is all for you, my love." Ryan dug into his dessert. The rest of the group followed his lead.

The guys insisted on cleaning up after dinner, but everyone pitched in. Soon the kitchen was clean and the dishwasher running. They went into the family room.

* * *

After talking for a few hours, Daniel noticed the time. "Hey guys, it's getting late. Ryan's letting me bunk at his house, and I need to get some sleep, so I can drive Becky back to college tomorrow."

Ryan smiled at Missy. "I hate to leave, but it's late. I'll see you tomorrow." He kissed her.

All the guys said "goodnight" as the girls watched from the front porch as they left.

Walking back inside, Missy asked Cissy, "Can you spend the night?"

"I'll need to call my parents to let them know. I don't have any pajamas, but maybe I can borrow a pair of yours." Cissy chuckled. "I think they'd fit, don't you?"

"I believe they will," Missy agreed with a laugh.

Cissy called her parents to let them know her plans. The twins and Becky talked till midnight before they went to bed.

Missy lay in bed just thinking. *It's been a wonderful day. How can I feel so happy when it's only been one day since I buried my parents and brother?* Missy prayed. "Dear Lord, I know they're with you. I hope they know I do miss them. You sent a miracle in my life by giving me back my sisters. I know you did this, Lord, and I thank you. Please see my heart and the things I'm confused about. Thanks for the comfort in my time of loss. My emotions are so mixed up. I feel happy, and then I'm guilty over these feelings. I know my parents would want me to go on with my life, but everything is happening so fast. Hold me in Your arms, Lord, and guide me as I move ahead with my new life. I know the scriptures say, 'Your word is a lamp to my feet and a light to my path.' I need your light guiding my path. In Jesus Christ's name. Amen."

Chapter 8

"Thanks for being here for me." Missy hugged Becky.

"You know I would've been here sooner if it hadn't been for my exams. I'll be back next weekend for the bridal shower."

"I can't believe it's so soon." Missy shook her head.

"The next months will fly by with your student teaching, finals, and wedding planning." Becky heard a car pull into the driveway and picked up her suitcase.

Missy touched her friend's arm. "You'll be here to help set up for the shower, right?"

"Yes," Becky assured her as the doorbell rang. "Well, got to go."

Missy opened the door and Daniel stood on the porch.

"Ready?" Daniel asked.

"Yes, here's my suitcase." Becky handed it to him and turned to Missy. "Have fun with Ryan."

"I plan to." Missy hugged her friend one last time.

"Hey," Cissy called out coming downstairs. "Don't leave without saying goodbye to me."

"I was wondering where you were." Becky reached her arms out to her new friend. "It's been great getting to know you."

"I hope we'll become good friends since I'm sure I'll be seeing you more."

"Plan on it." Becky hugged Cissy then turned to Missy. "Call me if there's anything I can do before the shower."

"I will," Missy replied. She watched as Becky and Daniel drove away. Then turned to her twin. "When do you need to leave?"

"Actually, now." Cissy took her keys out of her purse.

"Oh," Missy said. "thanks for staying last night."

"I had fun. We'll get together soon."

"I want you to come to my bridal shower. I'll call our sisters and invite them too."

Cissy gave her twin a hug. "I'd love to come. Now, I need to head home, so I can change before I go to work. They gave me a couple of days off, so I could be with you, but I don't want to take advantage of their generosity."

Missy opened the door and watched her sister walk to her car. She gave a little wave as Cissy backed out of the driveway. Standing on the porch, Missy realized she was alone again and started feeling uneasy, but Ryan arrived before it overtook her emotions.

"I'm sorry, I didn't get here before Becky and

Daniel left. I called my first sergeant and I have to leave in two days."

"I thought you had a week." Missy moaned as they walked to the family room.

"My week included the travel time and it took me longer to get home then I expected." Ryan took Missy's hand. "Sweetheart, I wanted to stay longer. That's why I called the sergeant and asked. He told me there's nothing he could do because you're not my immediate family, not yet anyway. I've told my parents I want to spend the next two days with you and they understand. Mom wants you to come to supper tonight. They still haven't been able to talk to you since all of this occurred. They wanted me to tell you how sorry they are for not being here when the accident happened. They were out of town until the night before the funerals."

"I knew they were gone, and your mother called when she heard the news. They tried to return home, but had problems getting an earlier flight." A tear trickled down her cheek. "I want to see them very much and would love to have supper with them. Your parents have always been like another set of parents to me since we started dating."

"We're so lucky to have each other and them." Ryan smiled. "My parents want to support you in any way they can while I'm gone."

"You're right. I'll need help finishing things for our wedding. Momma is . . . ah . . . was planning most of the details, and I don't think I can do this alone."

"Sweetheart, you'll have help. Mom already told me your mother discussed all the details with her, so she knows what's left to be done. Plus, you now have four sisters who I suspect will want to help. I think our wedding party just got bigger or am I mistaken?"

"No, you're right. I did ask my sisters to be bridesmaids. I hope you don't mind."

"Why would I mind? They're family and should be included."

"I don't know, silly me." Missy smiled. "I had a dream the other night and they stood at the altar beside Becky and you, waiting for me to walk down the aisle."

"Sounds like you have it worked out." Ryan chuckled. "Yes, Sweetheart, I like the idea to include your sisters in our special day. I'll need to come up with a few more groomsmen. I'll be standing at the altar waiting for you to become my bride before you realize it." Ryan kissed her gently and gave her a hug. He silently prayed, *God, please be with Missy these next few months while I'm away. She's your child, and right now, I don't think she feels she really belongs to anyone. Help her feel my love while I am away. I'm trusting in You, dear Lord, to bring all of us through this time of separation. I love her, Lord, and need her to trust in our love as she trusts in Your love. Give her the reassurance she needs.*

Ryan kissed her again and held her tightly. "My love for you is more than I can possibly tell you in words."

Missy looked into his eyes and smiled. "I love

you, Ryan, and am grateful God gave you to me."

Ryan kissed her again and slowly released her. He took a deep breath. "Hey, we need to stop this before I forget you're not my wife yet."

Missy blushed and smiled. "Just keep these thoughts for another four months and then we'll pick up from here."

"I'll hold you to it." Ryan took her hand. "So, what do you have to do today?"

"I'm not planning anything other than being with you. I'll be going back to my student teaching on Monday. My professor understands and told me to call her when I'm ready to come back. With you leaving this weekend, I don't see why I shouldn't go back on Monday."

"Don't push too fast, Missy. Grief affects people differently, and I don't think you have to rush back."

"I know, but this house will be very empty and quiet when you leave. I felt it this morning after everyone left. I was almost in tears just thinking about it when you drove up."

"Tears may be the best thing for you right now. You didn't have time to grieve before you learned of your sisters."

"I existed for four days after the accident without Becky or my sisters. I had people from church dropping by, my girls from Sunday school, and friends of my parents and David. I guess I didn't have time to be by myself and mourn their deaths except at night. I did a lot of crying, and then I had the awful dream of being alone."

"I didn't mean you needed to be by yourself. Sometimes just having someone in the house and letting you grieve in your own way is best. I know you, Sweetheart, you won't do well by yourself. This really bothers me more than anything right now." Ryan frowned, then his eyes brightened. "I have an idea; do you think Cissy would move in with you until we get married?"

"Cissy, stay here? Ryan, she has her own life. I can't ask her to move in here because I'm scared to be alone."

"You can ask. I have a feeling she'd do it, too."

"You really think so? I like my twin sister, and having her here the last few days has made me feel close to her."

"The only way you'll know for sure is to ask."

"Okay, I will, but I still feel it's silly to disrupt her life because of my fears."

"Missy, ask her." Ryan pulled out his cell phone. "Here, call her right now. Do you know her number?"

"Yes."

"Good, I do too." He dialed the number and handed the phone to Missy.

She took a deep breath before she spoke. "Hello, this is Missy."

"Is everything okay?" Cissy asked.

"Yes, but Ryan and I have been talking and . . . and . . . well . . ."

"What is it?"

"I'm going to ask you for a huge favor. If you can't do it, it's okay, but you see . . ." Missy looked at her fiancé and continued. "Ryan leaves in two days and then I'll be alone in the house and I am sort of wondering if . . ."

"Do you need me to come and stay with you for a while?"

Missy exhaled with relief. "Yes, please." She smiled. "Do you remember when Dottie told us about me not wanting to be alone after our father died? Well, I am feeling that way now. If you can't come and stay until the wedding, it's okay. I'll manage."

"Missy, I'd love to stay with you. I need to talk with my parents first, but I'm sure it'll be fine with them. It's not like I'm moving away forever or very far away. I'll call you back after I've talked to them. Okay?"

"Okay. Thank you."

"No problem, Sis. I think it's a great idea. Hey, I can even help with the wedding plans, if you want."

"I can use your help. Ryan's mother knows what's left to be done. Call back soon. Bye."

Missy looked at Ryan with tears in her eyes. "She's going talk with her parents, but it sounds like she'll come and stay with me."

"See, what did I tell you?" Ryan took the phone from her. "By the time I get back, you two will know everything about one another and hopefully rekindle the twin connection."

"I think we've been connecting already. At the spa, I found myself knowing what she'd say next. It's a strange feeling looking at her and seeing me and knowing how she would respond to certain things is eerie, but it feels right. Do you know what I mean?"

"No, not exactly, since I don't have a twin, but I can imagine how strange it might make you feel." Ryan chuckled. "Maybe being with Cissy daily will help you in more ways than then you think."

Missy took Ryan's hand. "Okay, now what are we going to do the next two days? All I want is to be with you as much as I can before you leave. Is there something you want to do while you're home?"

"No, nothing in particular."

"How about getting a picnic lunch and go to the park like we used to?"

"It sounds great, but have you looked at the weather outside? It's winter," Ryan said with a grin. "We can have a picnic, but it'll have to be inside,"

Missy laughed. "I forgot all about it being winter."

* * *

Missy and Ryan spent every waking hour possible with each other and talked a lot about their future.

"Ryan, do you think we should buy a house of our own, or stay here?"

"What do you want?" Ryan asked.

"I love this house, but it was Momma and Daddy's. I'd like to have a home to call our own after we're married."

"How about we do this. We'll stay here until we find the perfect house for us."

"Oh, Ryan, I love your idea. It'll give us time to look around." Missy's eyes pooled with tears. "I'll be going through things while you're gone, but I'll need your help to decide what to keep and what to give away."

Ryan took her hands. "Don't do it by yourself. If you want to wait until I return, we'll do it together."

Missy nodded her head. "Thanks, but I think I'll need to start with their clothes. I'll donate them to the homeless shelter."

"Sounds like you've already been thinking of what needs to be done."

Missy nodded. "I also need to do something with the cars."

"Your dad's car was totaled, so you'll be getting an insurance check for it. What are you thinking?"

"Momma's car is only a year old, so I'll keep it. I have a girl in my Sunday school class who has her driver's license but can't afford a car. So, I'm thinking of giving her my car. What do you think?"

"You should talk to her parents first. They may not want her to have a car yet."

"I never thought of that. I know she rides the bus to school and she has a job she walks to which takes her thirty minutes. I just thought it would help her."

"It would, but can they afford the insurance on

the car?"

"I don't know. I'll talk to her parents."

"What about David's car?"

"Sell it, maybe." Missy looked down at their hands as she blinked away the tears. "All of it will be hard, but I think it'll help me grieve. Cissy will be here to help with it, and I can share stories of my life with her."

"It will be healing, too." Ryan raised their entwined hands to his lips and kissed hers. "I'm so glad Cissy will be here with you while I'm gone."

"Me, too." She smiled and sighed. "I love you so much."

"You're the love of my life." He took her in his arms and kissed her. "Soon you'll be my bride."

"I hope our wedding will be as Momma and I planned."

"It will be."

"Thinking about it makes me happy and sad because Momma won't be there."

"She will be here in spirit," Ryan told her. "Besides, Mom has your mother's book she put together for the wedding. Our day will have her touches in everything."

Missy smiled. "I was thinking about the book and knew I needed to find it. I'm glad your mom has it." *Thank you, Momma, for everything you've done for me all my life.*

Chapter 9

The day arrived to say goodbye to Ryan. Missy stood back from the luggage check-in area and waited for Ryan. *Ryan's leaving. God help me be strong and show him I'll be okay while he's gone. He knows it's hard for me. Give me the strength to keep standing and smiling.*

With his duffle in hand, Ryan stood by Missy's side. "I'll be back," He wiped the tears from his fiancée's eyes, then took her in his arms. "It's less than four months, and God will be with you while I'm gone." He pressed a long, sweet goodbye kiss on Missy's lips, and then turned to walk down the ramp to board the plane.

Missy drove home blinking away tears and trying not to think how she felt. *Cissy's coming today to stay until Ryan comes home. It's going to be okay.* Then she said out loud, "I sure miss you, Momma. I could always talk to you about things." Tears filled her eyes and she quickly blinked them away. "Oh, I miss all of you so much." Her sadness grew as the emptiness filled her heart and she grieved for her family.

Arriving at her home, Missy sat in the car for

a few minutes to avoid going into the empty house. She reflected on the events of the past two weeks. Her throat tightened with a sob as she thought about how different her life would be. She could only rely on God being with her during those changes. She looked forward to becoming a wife, but the four months until her wedding weighed heavily on her mind. *How can I get through the days ahead?*

Sitting in this car isn't helping. She slowly opened the car door, got out, and walked to the front door. She looked around. *The reporters are gone and even the black truck. Thank you, Jesus.* She put the key into the lock and realized the door was unlocked. She frowned. *I know I locked the door. Why is it open? Oh, maybe Cissy is already here. Wait, no, I haven't given her the keys, yet. Maybe I didn't lock it because I was in a hurry to get to Ryan.* As Missy stepped into the house, she heard a car, and turned to see Cissy pulling into the driveway.

Cissy got out of her car, grabbed her suitcase and came to the door. "What's up?"

"I'm not sure. The door was unlocked. I know I locked it when I left to take Ryan to the airport."

Cissy took her sister's arm, "Let's go back to the car and call the police. Someone may be in there."

Missy pulled out her cell phone as they walked back to her car. She called 911 and explained to the operator someone may be in her house and wanted the police to come and check. Within a few minutes the police arrived and when Matt Stone, the Chief of Police, exited one of the cars with a patrolman, Missy told Cissy, "This is surprising; Chief Stone himself coming in response to my call." Another official vehicle arrived with two more policemen.

"Hello, Missy. What's this about an intruder?" the chief asked.

"I returned after taking my fiancé to the airport and found the front door unlocked."

Chief Stone told the detective and the policemen to go check the house. He turned back to Missy. "Are you sure you locked the door?"

"I'm pretty sure. It's a habit, but my mind was on Ryan leaving this morning, so maybe I didn't." Missy saw the look of confusion on the chief's face while looking at Cissy. "Chief, this is my twin sister, Cissy. It's a long story. Why did you come in response to my call?"

"Your father was a dear friend of mine, and I wanted to keep my eye on you. So, when I heard the call, I came to check everything myself." The chief paused for a moment. "I also, didn't get back in touch with you regarding the black truck, and I wanted to assure you we're looking into it. Have you seen it in the past few days?"

"No. I haven't seen it since the day of the funerals, but I haven't really looked either. Thanks for sending the patrol car to sit outside. It gave me peace of mind and a feeling of safety." Missy smiled and looked toward the house. "Do you think the person in the black truck is in there?"

"No, I don't." The detective came out of the

house, pulled the chief aside, and spoke in a low voice. The chief turned to Missy. "The house is empty but there's something the detective saw which didn't seem right, and I need you to look at it."

The twins followed the chief and detective into the house and up the stairs to the master bedroom. Missy looked around but at first didn't see anything out of place. Then she noticed a drawer in the desk was open. She walked to the desk and before she could touch it, the detective asked her not to touch anything.

"I know this drawer was closed and locked," Missy stated.

The chief nodded. "Was the key kept in the desk?"

"No, the key's in my room with Dad's belongings from the hospital," replied Missy.

The detective moved to the closet, opened the door, and motioned for Missy to look inside.

She saw some of the contents of the file cabinet on the floor. "Someone's gone through the files in Daddy's cabinet, but why?"

The chief took Missy's arm and led her out of the room. "We'll get to the bottom of this, but for now, I don't think it's safe for you to be here alone."

"I'm her roommate until her wedding," Cissy told him.

"Well, I think it's better right now if both of you stay somewhere else until my detectives can get all of the evidence and look into what is going on. Is there someplace you can go for a few days?" the chief asked.

Cissy took out her phone. "I'll call my mom. I'm sure it'll be okay if she stays at my house for a few nights."

"Oh, Cissy, are you sure?" Missy asked.

"Yes. Mom asked this morning when she'd be able to meet you. Spending a few days there will give her the opportunity to get to know you a little bit." Cissy went downstairs to make the call.

"Okay, Chief, but you'll let me know as soon as I can come back home, right?"

"Of course. It shouldn't take more than a day or so. I want to have your house dusted for fingerprints and look for other evidence to help us find out who did this and why. Now, go pack a bag. I'll make sure everything is locked up after the crime scene's been checked."

Cissy returned, smiling. "Mom said she'd be happy to have you at the house. I knew she would. Let's get you packed."

Missy looked around her bedroom, but nothing seemed out of place. She got her small bag out of her closet.

"What do you think the person wanted?" Cissy asked as she sat on the bed. "It wasn't a burglary, because it doesn't look like anything was taken or disturbed, except the file cabinet and desk drawer. Do you know if anything valuable was in it?"

"Not really. Becky went through it to find the investment files but found my adoption papers the day

I met you. After the lawyer brought the papers back, she returned them to the cabinet and locked it." Missy shook her head, "I haven't had time to go through it myself. So, I don't know all the contents. I have no idea what someone could've been looking for."

The chief knocked on the bedroom door. "Missy, are you ready to go?"

She nodded. "What do you think they were looking for? I don't think there was money or anything of value in the cabinet."

"We'll find out." The chief shook his head. "Just let us do our job, and we'll get the answers to your questions. I'd suggest the locks be changed. I'll have someone come by this afternoon, change them, and I'll bring you the new keys later."

"Thanks." Missy picked up her bag. "I was wondering if I needed to do that."

"Missy let me do this. I want to make sure you'll be safe."

"I'm very grateful for your taking control of this situation."

The chief led them out of the house and watched them pull onto the street before he took out his phone and made a call. Todd Horton, the marshal of Wichita County, answered after the first ring. "Horton, Stone here. There's been a break-in at the Calhoun house."

"Where's Missy?" Horton asked.

"She's going to stay at her sister's house."

"What did you tell her?"

"Nothing. I told her it'd take a few days to clear

the crime scene."

"Was she suspicious?"

"She asked questions, but I put her off."

"I'll be there in a few minutes. Start getting fingerprints."

"Okay, Marshal." The chief hung up.

Chapter 10

"Oh, my goodness, Missy, you're so much like Cassandra, but different." Mrs. Miles embraced Missy. "I'm so sorry for what you're going through. I've been praying for you since I heard of your situation."

Missy released the hug. "Thank you. It's very nice of you to let me stay here for a few days."

"I've wanted to meet you ever since my daughter told me about you, but not under these circumstances." Mrs. Miles gave an uncertain smile. "When we adopted her, we weren't told she had sisters nor a twin. I wished we'd known because we could have adopted both of you."

Missy smiled and looked at Cissy. "I wonder what it would've been like growing up with you. I've already learned we have so much in common, but having a sister to share things with would've made growing up so different." She looked at Mrs. Miles. "Don't misunderstand me, my parents and brother were wonderful and loving. But I always felt a loneliness which I now see was caused by our twin connection being torn apart."

"I agree." Cissy took Missy's hand. "Since I've been getting to know our sisters this past year, I've put together some of the missing pieces of the puzzle, but it always seemed unfinished. Now you're the last piece. It's amazing the inner peace I've had since we've met and thank God, I have all my sisters back in my life."

Missy smiled but there were tears in her eyes.

Cissy knew Missy was thinking of her parents and brother. She dropped her twin's hand and wrapped her arms around her and whispered, "I'm so sorry. I didn't mean to make you cry again. I only meant I'm glad you're in my life, but I'm so sorry how this came about."

"I know, it's just so hard not to cry when I think about them." Missy brushed away tears running down her cheeks. "I miss my parents and brother so much and wish you could have known them."

"Missy, it'll take a while to get over this tragedy and crying helps you grieve." Mrs. Miles handed her a tissue. "Try to think of the love they gave you and the good times, not the sad." She gently caressed Missy's arm. "Now, let's get you settled in the guest room."

"Thanks, Mom." Cissy took her sister's bag. "This way. We're going to have fun catching up. I can show you the scrapbooks Mom made for me. She always told me, I'd enjoy sharing them someday, and it looks like you are the one to show them to." She headed toward the bedrooms.

"Thank you, Mrs. Miles," Missy said over her

shoulder as she followed her twin down the hall.

* * *

Marshal Horton arrived at the Calhoun's house where the chief waited outside for him. He could see the area was secured.

"Marshal." Chief Stone nodded. "We've only found a few fingerprints, and I'm pretty sure they belong to the family. One set may be Missy's friend, Becky, since she opened the file cabinet the day before the funeral. We'll be asking for her fingerprints, so we can rule them out. I'll need to get the family's prints from you."

"Okay, I'll have my office fax them over to you as soon as possible. I'm more interested in the laptop. Do you have it?"

"No, we haven't found one. I'll have to ask Missy about it. Are you sure the information you need will be on the laptop?" The chief turned and entered the house.

Marshal Horton followed. "Yes, I spoke with Mr. Calhoun the afternoon of his death. He told me he'd obtained the information, and I'd planned to meet him the next morning. I think it's on his laptop. So, if you haven't found one, I assume it's been stolen, and our case is down the drain. Without what he recorded, we'll have to find another way to get the evidence needed to arrest Simon Delgado." He looked around the room. "Please call Missy and find out if she knows anything. If I need to meet with her to explain things, I will. But if you can get the location of the laptop over the phone, it'll keep her out of any more danger."

"Okay, I'll call her. Are you sure she doesn't know what her father was doing?" The chief pulled out his cell phone.

"According to her father, he hadn't told anyone because of the danger. He only talked to me about the case. Mr. Calhoun was a very courageous man by helping me bring down Delgado. We're about ready to arrest him but need the information in our hands before we do, so our case against him will be firm."

"Let me call Missy." The chief punched in the number. It rang a couple of times before she answered. "Missy, this is Chief Stone."

"Oh, did you find something?"

"The detectives are going through the house and want to make sure nothing is missing. As far as we can tell, all the electronics are here, but we didn't find any computers. Did your father bring his laptop home or leave it at his office? And do you have one? We just want to list everything which may have been taken."

"Daddy's laptop is in the house, but you won't find it, and mine's in the window seat in my room. I'll need to come over to make sure his is still there."

"Just tell me where it is, and I'll look," the chief declared. He didn't want her to return to the house with the marshal there.

"It's in a secret compartment. I'd promised

Daddy a long time ago I'd never tell anyone about it. I don't want to break my promise, especially now. I'll come over and get it for you."

"Okay, but have Cissy come with you. We need to get her fingerprints and, of course, we'll need yours, too." the chief looked at the marshal.

The marshal nodded in agreement knowing Missy would need to be told what was going on.

* * *

Within half an hour, the twins arrived at the house. Missy saw police cars and the black truck parked at the curb, but it was empty. She looked at Cissy. "Do you think a reporter is here?"

Cissy shrugged and followed her sister into the house.

They found Chief Stone talking with another man they'd never seen before.

"Good, you're here." Chief Stone gestured to the marshal. "Missy, this is the marshal of Wichita County, Todd Horton. He's working on a case which may have something to do with your situation, and, yes, he's the owner of the black truck you've seen in front of your house."

"Is my break-in more than just a simple robbery?" asked Missy.

"Miss Calhoun, my involvement in this case is a long story and not for everyone to hear." The marshal looked around at all the people in the room. "I've been watching your house, hoping to keep you safe. When I saw you leave this morning with your fiancé, I went to my office and hoped to get back here before you returned, but I was delayed. I'm sorry, I should've stayed here."

Missy looked from the marshal to the chief. "There's something you're not telling me. What is this all about?"

"Miss Calhoun, you'll be told when the time comes, but we need to know right now if your father's laptop is safe." Marshal Horton looked toward the stairs. "Could you please get it for us?"

"I don't know what all of this is about, but I'll do as you ask," Missy replied. "I'd like its location to be kept a secret, so if you could have your men leave my parents' room."

The marshal nodded to the chief, and they all went upstairs.

The chief spoke to the detectives, "I need all of you to take a break for a minute or two." He watched them as they left to go downstairs.

Missy moved into the bedroom, closed the door, and looked around. *Fingerprint dust everywhere.* She sighed, "Oh my, what a mess." She turned to the dresser, pulled out a drawer, and found a button to release the secret compartment. She picked up the laptop, closed the cubbyhole, and walked back into the hall. "Here's Daddy's laptop. Why do you need it?" she asked while handing it to the marshal.

"Thank you." The marshal took it. "I think

there's important information on it which will help with a case I've been working on for some time. With the help of your father, I'll have the evidence needed to put a person in prison for a very long time. If the information is here." The marshal held up the laptop. "By any chance, was there anything else with it?"

"No, it's the only thing there." Missy looked between the two men. "I hope you'll be able to tell me more about this case after the information is retrieved." She paused then asked, "Am I in danger?"

"You could be. Until this case is closed, anyone who knows about the laptop can be in danger," the marshal stated. "So, I'll have a policewoman stay with you for a few days after you return home, but I don't think anything will happen now since the laptop is going to be removed."

"But how will the person behind this know it's no longer here?" Missy asked.

"That's a good point, young lady. I think the culprit will have eyes on what's going on. I plan to take the laptop out myself in full view of everyone to show it's in my hands." The marshal tucked it under his arm, descended the stairs, and went out the front door.

Missy looked at the chief. "What's going on?"

"Like the marshal said, I can't talk about it right now, but know this, your father did a courageous thing by helping him. I'll take every precaution to keep you safe until the danger is over. Since the marshal is taking the laptop, the processing of the crime scene should be finished by tomorrow morning, then you can come back home. Right now, I need your fingerprints and yours, too, Cissy. Also, will you give me Becky's phone number? She'll have to go to the police station, so her fingerprints can be taken. We have to rule out everyone we know who's been in the house to find the prints which don't belong."

"We weren't the only people in the house since the death of my family," Missy revealed, "but only Becky and I went into my parents' room. There were ladies from church, my lawyer's associate, Becky's fiancé, Daniel, Ryan, and all my sisters were downstairs. Will you need all their fingerprints?"

"Maybe, but right now we are concentrating on your parents' room. If we extend the fingerprinting to other rooms, I'll need names of the people then, but I'll let you know." The chief lightly touched Missy's shoulder. "I'm sorry I can't tell you any more right now."

"Daddy always said I could depend on you if I needed to." Missy smiled. "There shouldn't be too many different fingerprints in the bedroom." She looked over at Cissy. "I think today was the first time my sister was in there."

Cissy nodded. "Yes, I've been upstairs, but not in there. I don't think I touched anything, because you said not to."

"Okay, but just in case, let's get your prints." The chief motioned for them to go downstairs. "Then you both can return to Cissy's home. I'll send a patrol car to watch your house tonight. Missy, tomorrow I'll bring you the new keys and let you know when it's okay for y'all to come home. Tonight, I'll have a policeman stay here to make sure there won't be another intruder."

"This is serious, isn't it?" Missy asked.

"Yes, it is. Now let's get those prints."

* * *

Missy was deep in thought on the drive to her sister's home.

"Are you okay?" Cissy asked.

"I'm sorry, I was thinking about the weeks before the accident. Daddy seemed nervous about something and he always needed to know where I was going and when I'd be home. It was as if he didn't want me or David out of his sight. I wasn't with them when the accident happened, because I'd volunteered to help the youth at church get ready for a mission trip. The pastor came to tell me about the accident. Momma told the EMT's where I could be found before she lost consciousness. She didn't make it to the hospital." Missy broke down.

Cissy took her hand and held it until Missy stopped crying.

"Missy, you can talk to me when you're ready. I'm a good listener."

"Oh, Cissy, what if it wasn't an accident? What if . . ."

"Don't think that way." Cissy squeezed her

twin's hand and looked in the rearview mirror. "We're here, so let's get inside. I don't know about you, but I feel like we're being watched."

Missy's eyes widened and her face paled. "Do you think we were followed? Could . . . could he still be after me even though the marshal has the laptop?"

Cissy shrugged. "I don't know, but I'd feel safer inside with my parents. They both jumped out and ran in the house.

* * *

The rest of the day and night was uneventful. Cissy made her sister laugh at some of the antics she'd done in her younger years.

Her parents kept shaking their heads and answering Missy's questions about her twin's childhood.

"Mr. and Mrs. Miles, I can't tell you how comfortable and safe I feel being in your home. It's been a stressful day and you've helped me relax. Thank you for sharing Cissy's past with me. I feel a connection with all of you. I see your love for her, and I'm so happy to spend this time here. Thank you also for letting her stay with me while Ryan's away." Missy yawned. "I'm sorry, but I need to get some rest."

"Yes, of course. You're worn out." Mrs. Miles stood. "It's been a long day. Tomorrow will be a new day."

Chapter 11

The next day, the chief called Missy. "I've had the locks changed, and we're through getting evidence. The fingerprint dust is cleaned, so it's okay for you and Cissy to return to the house. Can you meet me there at three?"

"Yes, we'll be there," Missy replied. "Chief, thanks for helping me."

"It's okay. Your family has always been special to me, so, it's more than just my job."

"Well, it's a comfort to know you're near in case I need you. See you later."

Missy found Cissy and her mom in the living room. "Cissy, the chief called and we're to meet him at the house at three. Is that okay?"

Cissy and her Mom looked at each other.

"Missy are you sure it's safe for y'all to go back to your house?" Mrs. Miles asked.

"Yes. The chief is having a policewoman stay with us for a few days." Missy smiled at her. "If you want Cissy to stay here, I understand."

"Oh, no, it's not that, Missy." Mrs. Miles stepped

over to her and put her hand on her shoulder. "I'm just concerned for the safety of both of you."

"Mom, we're going to be fine," Cissy said.

"Promise me you'll call tonight before you go to bed." She hugged her daughter.

"Okay, Mom, I will."

* * *

As Cissy drove to meet the chief, she kept looking in the rearview mirror.

"What are you doing?" Missy asked.

"I'm making sure we aren't being followed." Cissy glanced again into the mirror.

"Are you scared?"

"Well, I'm a little nervous. Aren't you?"

"I guess I am now if I think about it." Missy nodded. "I've been praying this morning, and I feel God is giving me the strength to do what's necessary to get through this. I must rely on Him to give me a feeling of safety."

"I think your prayers are working." Cissy smiled. "There's a police car behind us, now. I feel safer already."

Cissy drove her car into Missy's driveway. The black truck and the chief's car were on the street.

Missy looked at her twin. "Something's wrong."

She nodded in agreement.

They walked into the house and saw the chief and the marshal in the middle of a conversation which stopped when they saw the girls.

"Missy," the marshal greeted her. "The information wasn't on the laptop or it's been deleted. My IT guy couldn't find any trace of it. Do you know if your father has another computer?"

"No." Missy shook her head. "This is the only one Daddy owns. He does have a computer at the bank. When are you going to tell me what's going on?"

"I guess you need to know, since you may be in danger," the marshal replied. "Please remember, this is an on-going investigation and what is said here will have to be kept in strictest confidence."

"I understand." Missy looked at Cissy who nodded in agreement.

"Let's sit down while I explain everything, so you'll know the extent of the severity of this situation."

"Let's talk in the family room." Missy motioned to the back of the house.

Once everyone found a seat the marshal cleared his throat. He looked at Missy. "This started about four months ago when we received information about a man trying to shift drug money into his business. He set up a dummy company in your father's bank. He's done this before in other cities, but I wasn't able to get the information from the other banks to implicate him."

"But Daddy got the information you needed?" Missy asked.

"Yes." The marshal nodded. "I had an undercover policeman working in your father's bank as a teller. He was to monitor the suspect's transactions. Unfortunately, he broke his leg and was unable to finish the assignment. So, your father said he'd get it and give it to me." The marshal looked at the chief then at Missy. "Your father told me he made a copy of the account's activities and a recording of some transactions. We'd planned to meet on the day after his accident occurred. We've determined the accident was suspicious."

"Suspicious?" Missy's eyes widened. "You mean it may have been intentional?"

The marshal hesitated a moment before answering. "Yes. The evidence from the accident is still being reviewed. So, as you can see, we are trying to keep you safe until the suspect can be arrested."

"What should I do?" Missy asked.

"I think you need to continue with your normal routine, but I want a policewoman with you at all times," the marshal stated.

"What have you planned to do for the next week or so?" the chief asked.

"I was going back to student teaching," Missy replied. "Then on Friday, there's a bridal shower planned, and it's here. Should I cancel it?"

"No." The marshal answered. "The bridal shower will give us a chance to get more undercover policewomen into the house without suspicion, if needed. I can have them come posing as guests, then they can stay here for your protection. Right now, though, the chief has one coming over to stay with you and go everywhere with you. When she comes, I need you to act as if she is a long-lost friend when you greet her at the door."

"Okay, but do you think I should tell the people coming to the shower about the danger?" Missy inquired.

"No, please be assured, we are taking every precaution to keep you safe," the marshal replied. "We'll have this house under surveillance, and if anyone suspicious comes around they'll be detained. I think we can protect you better here than anywhere else, plus you'll be able to go through your parents' things to look for anything we might have missed. I'm sure it's in this house," the marshal stated.

"Okay." Missy looked at her twin. "I'm so sorry to put you in this situation."

"I wouldn't want to be any other place now," Cissy told her sister. She moved over on the couch to wrap her arms around her. "I'm here for you."

"I guess we need to leave." The chief stood. "Be expecting Juanita, the policewoman, to come to the door shortly. I wanted her to arrive after we left, so there wouldn't be a connection to the police." The chief put his hand on Missy's shoulder. "You'll be safe here. Juanita is excellent at her job and has experience in protecting people. Listen to her, she knows how to keep you safe. You have my cell number, so call me if you have any problems or feel uneasy about anything." The chief handed the new house keys to her.

"Okay, Chief." Missy nodded as she took the

keys.

After the chief of police and the marshal left, Missy looked around the house and didn't see anything out of place. She walked into each room but felt a little uneasy.

Cissy sensed her twin's feelings and tried to get her mind off what they'd learned. "You said there's a bridal shower for you on Friday?"

Missy nodded.

"Is there anything I can do to help get ready for it?"

Missy looked at Cissy with sad eyes. "Momma planned the shower with Ryan's mom. I should probably call her to find out the plans." She shook her head. "I can't believe this is happening. Daddy's involved with an undercover operation with the marshal's office and it may have been the reason they died." Missy fell into a chair and sighed. "I am so confused and afraid."

Cissy took her twin's hands. "It sounds like your father was a man of integrity and wanted to do what was right. We need to believe the marshal will get the evidence and arrest the one who is responsible for all this."

"But . . ." The doorbell rang. She started shaking.

Cissy took her by the shoulders. "It's just Juanita. Remember what Chief Stone said. You're supposed to greet her as a friend. Okay?"

Missy nodded and walked to the front door. She could see a young woman standing outside with a suitcase. She opened the door with a smile on her face. "Juanita!"

Juanita stepped forward, gave Missy a hug, and whispered in her ear, "Very good, now let's get indoors."

Missy stepped back and let the policewoman inside. She closed the door and turned to her sister and introduced them.

"Wow! How am I going to tell you two apart?" Juanita asked.

Missy looked at her twin and shrugged.

"Well, for one thing, if you look close, I have a scar at my right ear where I fell when I was little." Cissy pointed to her ear.

Juanita smiled and nodded. "I can see it now. Thanks. Let's get acquainted, and I'll tell you what my part in this is going to be."

The twins nodded, and Missy led the way into the family room.

"I'm here for your protection. So, I'll be going everywhere with you." Juanita looked at the twins. "Tell me what you'll be doing tomorrow."

"I start my student teaching," Missy answered.

"What about you, Cissy?" Juanita asked.

"I work at a day care during the day, and I have classes at night," Cissy replied.

"Well, I guess we'll drop Cissy off at work and then we'll go to the school." Juanita looked at Cissy. "I'll call the chief to have someone watch the day care."

"But it's Missy you're supposed to keep safe, right?" Cissy looked between the two.

"We can't take any chances. Because you're identical, we don't want anything to happen to you by mistake," Juanita said. "We need to act like we're long-time friends while in public. Then when we are here, I'll be setting up surveillance around the house."

"On Friday, there's a bridal shower planned for me." Missy looked at Juanita. "It's to be held here."

"I'll need a list of the guests." Juanita took a pad out of her pocket.

"I don't have it, but my fiancé's mother does; she helped plan it." Missy picked up the phone. "Should she come over here in person to give you the details?"

"Yes." Juanita nodded. "I also need to know any other people who may be coming such as a caterer, florist, or photographer."

"I don't know if she hired them, but I'll find out." Missy hit the speed dial on her phone.

"Hi, Mrs. Franklin, it's Missy," she said when her future mother-in-law answered.

"Are you okay?"

"Yes." Missy tried to lighten her tone. "I'm wondering about the bridal shower on Friday. Is it still going to happen?"

"I was going to call and ask if you wanted to cancel."

"No," Missy said quickly and looked at Juanita. "I mean, I think it'll be good for me to go ahead with it. You know, to get my mind on the future."

"Oh, sweetie, I know it's hard for you, and I was hoping you wouldn't cancel. I do think it'll be good for you to be with your friends and celebrate something happy."

"May I add a couple of friends to the list?" Missy looked at Juanita. "Could you come over with the details of the shower and the guest list?"

"Yes. When do you want me to come?"

"I was hoping you could come over for a light supper. Nothing fancy, just sandwiches," Missy replied.

"Let me gather everything and I'll be there in about an hour. Okay?"

"Great. Thanks for doing this." Missy nodded to Juanita. "I'll see you in a little while."

"Missy, remember we love you. Bye, dear."

Missy ended the call and looked at Juanita. "She's coming over within the hour and needs to be told what's going on."

"Yes, I'll explain it to her when she gets here. It gives me time to look over the house and set up some equipment." Juanita stood.

"I'll show you where you'll sleep." Missy led the way to the stairs. "It's my brother's room."

"I'll also need to see your parents' room. I've been told it was the only one ransacked. I'm to set up surveillance cameras in there, the hallways, garage, and all doors leading outside," Juanita stated as she followed Missy down the hallway.

"Do you want me to show you around or do you want to look on your own?" Missy asked.

They reached her brother's room.

"If you don't mind, I'd prefer to look on my

own." Juanita put her suitcase on the bed.

"Just let me know if you need anything." Missy glanced around her brother's room. Tears filled her eyes.

"Are you okay, Missy?" Juanita asked.

"Sorry." She wiped her eyes. "It's so hard to believe all of this has happened. It's only been two weeks since I lost everyone, and with everything going on, I haven't really been able to grieve. It's hard being in here."

"I can't tell you I know what you're going through, because I don't. I still have my family. I'll try to make the time I'm here easy on you." Juanita stepped closer to Missy. "I've been told I'm a good listener, so if you just want to talk, I'll listen."

Missy nodded and tried to smile. "Thank you."

"Now, let me get started before Mrs. Franklin gets here."

"I'll go set the table and get supper ready for all of us." Missy turned and walked out of the room.

* * *

The twins were putting the ham and turkey on a platter for sandwiches when the doorbell rang.

Juanita came down the stairs, stopped Missy in the hallway, and whispered. "Before you open the door, look to see who it is. If you don't know them, I'll answer the door."

Missy went to the door, looked out the side

window, saw her future mother-in-law standing on the porch, and glanced at Juanita. "It's Mrs. Franklin."

Juanita nodded.

Missy opened the door with a smile. "Hello, perfect timing. I just put everything on the table for all of us."

"Us? Who else is here?" Mrs. Franklin entered the house and looked at Juanita.

"Um, this is Juanita." Missy closed the door.

"It's a pleasure to meet you." Juanita extended her hand.

"Nice to meet you, too." Mrs. Franklin took Juanita's hand and looked at Missy. "Is she who you wanted to add to the guest list?"

"Well, sort of. Juanita is really an undercover policewoman." Missy saw the alarm on her future mother-in-law's face. "Let's go to the table, and she can explain why she's here."

"Oh, my goodness." Mrs. Franklin followed them into the dining room.

"I'm sure Ryan told you about Cissy, my twin sister," Missy stated as they entered the dining room where she waited for them.

"Yes, he did tell me, and I finally get to meet you, Cissy." Mrs. Franklin nodded.

"Nice to meet you." Cissy shook her hand.

"I'm going to have to find a way to tell you two apart." Mrs. Franklin looked between the twins.

They both giggled and explained what to look for.

"Let's eat while Juanita explains everything." Missy motioned to the table and reached for her sister's and future mother-in-law's hand. They, in turn, took Juanita's hand.

"Let's pray." Missy bowed her head. "Dear Lord, I praise you for everything you are doing for me in this storm. I thank you for protecting me. I pray for Your guidance in the coming days. Bless this food and the ones who share it with me. In Jesus Christ's name. Amen." Missy squeezed both hands.

Mrs. Franklin looked at Missy. "I don't think I can eat until I know what's going on."

"It's okay." Missy looked across the table at Juanita. "Juanita, will you explain, please?"

"Yes. I know this isn't what you were expecting when you came here today." Juanita took a sip of water. "There was a break-in when Missy took Ryan to the airport. Chief Stone and Marshal Horton believe it has something to do with the investigation Missy's father was part of."

"Oh, Missy, I'm glad you weren't here," Mrs. Franklin said, then looked at Juanita. "Investigation?"

"Mr. Calhoun was getting bank information about a man suspected of money laundering. He'd set a time to meet Marshal Horton which was supposed to be the day after the accident. We believe the man thinks there's something in this house which can incriminate him." Juanita looked at Missy. "We suspect he broke into the house to look for it, but we don't have proof as of yet."

"Do you think he'll break in again?" Mrs. Franklin asked.

"We assume he will to continue his search. I'm here to keep them safe and keep the house under surveillance. I'll go everywhere with Missy."

"They're in danger?" Mrs. Franklin asked and took Missy's hand again.

"I don't think so." Juanita smiled. "This is just a precaution, and hopefully, it'll prevent another break-in."

"Missy, do you want to come and stay at my house until this man is caught?" Mrs. Franklin asked.

"Marshal Horton thinks I should continue with my normal routine with Juanita's protection." Missy patted Mrs. Franklin's hand. "I'm sorry you've been dragged into this situation."

"Don't worry about me, dear." Mrs. Franklin let go of Missy's hand. "It's you and Cissy I'm worried about."

"I assure you," Juanita said, "I'll do everything in my power to keep them safe. It's the reason you needed to know the situation."

"I'm glad you told me." Mrs. Franklin smiled nervously. "I can't do anything to help protect them, but I can pray for this situation."

"It's also why I need to know who'll be coming this Friday to the bridal shower." Juanita smiled at Mrs. Franklin. "There'll be a couple of undercover policewomen who will come and blend in with the guests but won't leave. They'll stay here day and night to monitor the house."

"I've got the list of who's been invited." She retrieved an envelope from her purse. "Not everyone has confirmed they're coming, but I marked the ones who did respond."

"That's great." Juanita took the envelope. "I'll also need to know if there's anyone you've hired who will be in and out of the house on Friday."

"A list of the people is in there also." Mrs. Franklin gestured to the envelope.

"Good." Juanita smiled. "This will help."

"Mrs. Franklin . . ." Missy started, but her future mother-in-law interrupted.

"Please call me Katie or, if you like, Mom."

"Oh, I would love to call you Katie," Missy replied. "But I don't think I can call you Mom, not yet."

"As you prefer. Now you were saying before I interrupted."

"I was just going to thank you for taking over everything my mom planned for the shower and wedding." Missy smiled.

"It's not a problem. Your mother wrote everything down and made copies for me so I'd know the plans. She gave me the book to review, but I didn't get it back to her before the . . . before the accident."

"I'm glad Momma was so organized." Missy looked at Juanita. "Is there anything else we need to discuss right now?"

Juanita shook her head. "I think this has everything I need." She placed the pages back in the envelope.

"I don't know about y'all, but I'm hungry, so let's eat." Missy picked up the plate of luncheon meat and passed it to Katie.

"I think I can eat a little now since I know what's going on, but my stomach is still in a knot." Katie took the plate and smiled at Missy.

So, the week began with a new friend in the house, a bodyguard.

Chapter 12

Missy looked out the window at the bright, sunny sky. "Oh, what a beautiful morning," she sang with a smile.

Cissy knocked on her sister's bedroom door. "I know you're awake, Missy, because I hear you singing."

Missy opened the door. "It's a beautiful morning!"

"Yes, it is, and you're in good spirits." Cissy hugged her twin.

"I'm a little excited about today."

"Isn't there a lot to do before the shower tonight?"

"No, I don't think so. Mrs. . . . ah . . . Katie will be here in a little while to get started with decorations. We dusted and vacuumed yesterday."

"Let's make breakfast before Mrs. Franklin puts us to work." Cissy turned toward the door.

"I'll be right down." Missy followed Cissy out of the bedroom. "I want to check with Juanita."

"Okay, ask if she wants breakfast with us or up here again," Cissy told her sister as she walked downstairs.

"I'll ask her and then come help." Missy turned to the room Juanita was staying in. She knocked on the door. No answer. She went to her parents' room where surveillance equipment was set up and knocked.

"Come in," Juanita responded.

"Good morning." Missy opened the door. "You're up early. How's it going?"

"Okay." Juanita looked up from the computer. "Everything's ready for tonight."

"Great." Missy walked over to where Juanita sat. "Cissy and I are going to cook breakfast. Do you want to eat with us or do you want me to bring you something up here?"

"I think I'll eat with y'all this morning." Juanita hit a few keys on the keyboard and stood. "I have it programed to record, and I can use a break. I've been up since about three this morning."

"Why were you up so early? Did something happen?"

Juanita held up her hand. "Everything's fine. I thought I heard something and got up to check. It was the neighbor's dog barking, so I took a look at the monitors. Didn't see anything at first, then I saw the dog barking at a squirrel walking along the fence. I couldn't go back to sleep." She walked into the hallway.

"Coffee is needed, I assume." Missy followed Juanita out the door and downstairs.

"Yes," Juanita agreed. "Lots of it."

The two of them entered the kitchen.

"I've got coffee on and bacon in the oven to go with eggs," Cissy said. "Hope it's okay with y'all."

"Yes, it sounds great." Missy opened the refrigerator. "If we make a good breakfast now, we can have a light lunch while decorating. I saw the caterer's menu for tonight and there's going to be lots of food."

"I agree." Cissy pulled a skillet out of the cabinet and put it on the stove. She looked at her twin and asked, "Do you want anything else?"

"Just some toast. Is this okay with you, Juanita?" Missy asked as she walked to the stove.

"Yes, it's fine." Juanita stretched. "I'll take a walk around the backyard and check out things while y'all are cooking."

"Looks like the coffee's done." Missy picked up a cup. "Juanita, do you want to take a cup with you?"

"Great. Caffeine and fresh air are what I need right now." Juanita took the cup from Missy and poured some.

"Do you want cream and sugar?" Missy opened the cabinet and grabbed the sugar.

"No." Juanita shook her head. "Not this morning. I need it strong."

"It's been a long day already for you, hasn't it?" Missy asked.

"Yes, thanks to the neighbor's dog." Juanita took her cup and headed out the back door. "See y'all in a few minutes."

"Missy, what happened last night?" Cissy asked.

"The dog next door woke her up early this

morning."

"Nothing else happened?"

"She said there wasn't anything else." Missy poured coffee into a cup and offered it to her sister. "I suspect she's checking the backyard to make sure she didn't miss anything."

"I'm glad she's being so diligent." Cissy took the cup. "I'm praying for everything to go smoothly tonight."

"Me, too." Missy added sugar to her cup and stirred. "I want this whole thing to be over, so I can feel safe again."

"Are you scared?" Cissy touched her twin's shoulder.

"Yes, I am." Missy frowned. "It's . . . well . . . just not knowing what's going to happen. Will this man try to break in again? Will he try to hurt us? Will he . . ."

"Missy, stop!" Cissy exclaimed. "You're only getting yourself worked up. The unknown is always scary, but you have God's protection, and Marshal Horton is doing everything to keep you safe. You know this."

"Yes, I do." Missy put her cup on the counter. "Sometimes all the events of the last few weeks feel like a dream. I want it to just go away, so I can get back to my old life." She held up her hand. "I know my situation is different now, but I haven't had a chance to think straight because of all the changes in my life."

Cissy encased her twin in a hug. "It'll get better with time. I know you're hurting, confused, and wondering how this happened to your family. I want to support you and be a good listener. I don't have any answers, but I know who does, God."

"Thank you." Missy gave a gentle squeeze and eased from the hug. "I guess I needed someone to share how I feel. You're such a great comfort to me."

"It's what sisters are for." Cissy turned around and peeked in the oven. "The bacon will be done in a few minutes."

"I'll start the eggs." Missy went to the refrigerator and took out the carton of eggs.

"Anytime you need to talk, I'm here."

"I'm so blessed."

Juanita entered and walked to the coffee pot. "Everything is normal out back. Great coffee, Cissy."

"Thanks. Breakfast should be ready in a few minutes."

They completed preparing breakfast and went into the dining room with their plates.

"Will you say a blessing for us?" Missy asked looking at her twin.

"Sure." Cissy joined hands with Missy and Juanita. "Dear Lord, thank you for this food and the company. I ask a special blessing on Missy this day and give us a good night with her friends. In Jesus Christ's name. Amen."

"So, what are the plans for today?" Juanita asked before taking a bite of eggs.

"We'll be getting the house ready for tonight." Missy sipped her orange juice. "Katie will arrive around ten, so we can start decorating. She has all the decorations, and I'm not sure what else she plans."

"Okay, I have the names of the policewomen coming tonight. They're Stephanie and Teresa." Juanita sipped her coffee. "They'll be dropped off down the street and walk to the house between 6:45 and 7:00. We don't want any cars left in the street after the guests leave tonight."

"I didn't think about extra cars if they drove." Missy spooned jam on her toast. "I do have neighborhood friends who are walking over, so it won't look unusual."

"Is Becky going to come?" Cissy asked.

"Yes, she'll be here." Missy took a bite of her eggs. "Becky's coming in today and will stay the weekend."

"Here?" Juanita asked.

"No, her parents live next door." Missy wiped her mouth with her napkin. "She'll be staying with them. She's aware of Cissy staying here with me, and she'll be over during the weekend."

"Does she know what's going on?" Juanita asked.

Missy shook her head. "I've only told her Cissy is staying with me while Ryan's away. I haven't told her about you being here. I may have to since she's going to be around this weekend."

"Let's wait and see." Juanita finished her juice. "The fewer people who know what's going on, the better."

"How will I explain you and the other policewomen being here?" Missy asked.

"They'll be upstairs and out of sight." Juanita stood. "I'll try to stay upstairs also when you have company."

"Okay, but what if we have to go out?" Missy pushed her chair back from the table and stood. "We have a fitting for our dresses tomorrow."

"I'll have to call the marshal and tell him we need to let Becky in on what's going on." Juanita picked up her plate. "I'll make the call now."

"Leave those in the sink." Cissy indicated the plate and glass. "I'll clean up."

"Thanks." Juanita left the dining room.

"Cissy, I'll help you." Missy picked up her dishes and started toward the kitchen.

"When do you think Becky will be here?" Cissy followed her sister.

"She told me she's leaving around nine this morning from Denton. It takes about an hour and forty-five minutes to get here." Missy looked at the clock. "So, in a couple of hours."

"Is she going to help us with the shower decorations?" Cissy set the dishes by the sink.

"Yes, of course." Missy chuckled. "Being my maid of honor, Becky plans to help with everything."

"It'll be good to see her again." Cissy ran water in the sink.

* * *

At about ten, the doorbell rang. Juanita ran down the stairs and stood by the front door.

Missy came out of the family room, walked toward the door, and nodded to Juanita before peeking out the window. "It's Katie."

"Okay." Juanita nodded.

Missy opened the door and greeted her future mother-in-law with a hug. "Come in. Isn't it a beautiful day?"

"Yes, and it's going to be a wonderful night." Katie stepped inside the house. "Good morning, Juanita."

"Good morning. Are there any changes to the details of the shower?"

"No, the florist should be delivering the flowers this afternoon. The caterer will be here around five to set up the food, and then they'll leave. The photographer is due at 6:30 to take a few pictures before the fun begins."

"It's good to know the times people will be arriving," Juanita said. "Do you need any help unloading decorations?"

"Yes, there are couple of boxes in the trunk. Thanks." Katie laid her purse on the hallway table. "I think the two of us can get them."

"I'll help you," Missy told Katie.

"No, you stay in the house," Juanita stated and walked to the door.

"Okay, but . . ."

"Missy, please, stay in the house. I'll help Mrs.

Franklin," Juanita interrupted.

Missy opened the door and looked at Juanita. "I'll do as you say." She watched as they retrieved the decorations from the car and returned to the house.

Missy held the door open for them. "Let's get started." She said as she closed the door.

Katie carried a box down the hallway to the family room with the others following. "I assume you want the shower held in here."

"Yes, it's bigger than the living room." Missy looked around. "There's more seating in here, but we'll still need to set up some folding chairs."

"I'm here to help, also," Cissy said as she entered. "Hi, Mrs. Franklin."

"Good morning. There's a lot to do, and your help will be appreciated."

"Tell me what you want done, and I'll do it." Cissy clapped her hands. "I love parties."

Mrs. Franklin looked around the room. "We need to get the folding chairs and place them around the room, so I can see how everything fits."

"Are the chairs in the garage?" Cissy asked.

"Yes, over by the shelves."

"I'll get them."

Missy took the box Juanita was still holding. "Thanks for helping with the boxes."

"You're welcome," she replied. "I'm going back upstairs if y'all don't need me."

"I think we can handle it." Mrs. Franklin smiled. "Thanks for all you're doing for Missy."

"It's my job." Juanita shrugged. "Besides, it's a pleasure getting to know Missy and Cissy. I've never been around twins before, and it's interesting how they know what the other is going to say or do sometimes."

"I'm still getting used to the fact I'm a twin." Missy shook her head. "It takes me by surprise a little when she says something I was thinking."

"I heard my name." Cissy entered the room carrying a couple of chairs. "What did I do now?"

"Nothing." Missy giggled. "I was telling Juanita how I'm still getting used to having a twin and the feelings I get when you do something I would do."

"Yeah." Cissy put down the chairs. "I know what you mean. It's creepy sometimes but in a good way."

"I hope there are more chairs in the garage," Mrs. Franklin declared. "With everyone who's attending, we'll need more seating."

"Yes, about eight more chairs out there." Cissy turned to go to the garage.

"I'll help you carry them in." Missy followed her twin.

"I'm going to get everything out of the boxes, so I can decide what needs to be done first." Mrs. Franklin took streamers, vases, table cloths, and party favors from the box.

* * *

Less than an hour later, the doorbell rang.

Juanita met Missy again in the front hallway.

"It's Becky," Missy stated looking out the window. She opened the door. "I'm so glad you're here."

"It's good to be here." Becky embraced Missy in a hug. "How are you doing?"

"I'm okay." Missy stepped back from the hug and closed the door. "Becky, I'd like you to meet Juanita."

"Hello." Becky extended her hand and looked puzzled.

Juanita shook her hand. "There's something you need to know."

"Missy?" Becky looked at her friend with worry lines on her forehead.

"It's a long story. Let's go into the family room. Cissy and Mrs. Franklin are decorating, and Juanita can explain what's going on."

The three women walked down the hallway into the family room.

Cissy let out a squeal when she saw Becky and ran to give her a hug. "Becky, you're here!"

Despite the enthusiastic greeting, Becky looked at Juanita with concern. "What do you have to tell me?"

Juanita walked to the chair and sat down and everyone else found a seat. "Missy hasn't told you what's happened since Ryan left, has she?"

"I know there was a break-in." Becky glanced at Missy. "I had to give my fingerprints, because I was in her parents' room."

"Yes." Missy nodded. "But there's more."

"Missy's father was helping with a police investigation." Juanita explained. "We believe the break-in is connected to what Mr. Calhoun found out."

"Oh, Missy." Becky touched her friend's hand. "Are you in danger?"

"No." Missy looked at Juanita. "Well, I don't think so."

Becky turned back to Juanita. "Who are you exactly?"

"I'm an undercover policewoman," Juanita said. "I'm here to protect these two for a while."

Becky gasped. "They are in danger."

Juanita shook her head. "It's a precautionary measure. We're doing everything possible to keep them safe."

"Please tell me everything."

Juanita told Becky details of the investigation, plans for the shower, and the weekend.

"Do you have any questions?" Juanita asked.

Becky looked at her friend. "I'm dumbfounded. How long will this protection continue?"

"Not sure." Juanita shook her head. "Once we find the file Mr. Calhoun retrieved for the marshal, we can arrest the man in question. Until then, we'll be here day and night."

"Are you going to cancel the shower?" Becky asked.

"No, we're using the shower to get two more policewomen into the house to help with surveillance."

Juanita stood. "If you have any other questions, I'll be upstairs monitoring the cameras around the house." She walked out of the room.

Becky turned to Missy. "Why haven't you told me what's going on?"

"The marshal asked me not to tell anyone until they needed to know." Missy shrugged. "I wanted to tell you everything when it happened. You're my best friend, and it was hard not talking to you about this."

"It's okay. I understand. So, now I know. How are you really doing?"

"I'm a little scared," Missy said glancing at her twin. "I'm glad Cissy's been here with me, and I can talk to her about it."

"Are you sure you want to go through with the shower?" Becky asked. "Won't the guests be in danger?"

Missy shook her head. "The marshal doesn't think anything will happen tonight with people here and, as Juanita said, it'll be cover for bringing in the other policewomen."

Mrs. Franklin stood and picked up a vase. "We're all concerned about this situation. I've tried to get them to stay with me until this is over, but Juanita seems to think they're safer here."

"Are you sure, Missy?" Becky asked.

"Yes." Missy nodded and looked around the room. "Let's not dwell on the 'what ifs' anymore. There's a party to get ready for."

"I can't even imagine how you're feeling, Missy," Mrs. Franklin said. "But I think it will be good to get all of our minds off the situation by finishing the decorations for tonight."

* * *

The shower guests arrived bringing an atmosphere of joy, good wishes, and presents. When the policewomen arrived, they carried gift-wrapped boxes and went straight upstairs to help Juanita. The guests didn't even know they were in the house.

Everyone laughed and shared how they met Missy and Ryan and how they knew the couple were made for each other. It was obvious everyone was looking forward to the wedding. But, after all the guests left, the reality of the situation in the house became apparent when the three policewomen came downstairs.

"Everything's okay, Missy." Juanita pointed to the other two policewomen. "I want to introduce you to Stephanie and Teresa."

"Hello." Missy shook each officer's hand. "This is my twin sister, Cissy. Before you ask, Cissy has a scar by her ear. It's how you can tell us apart."

"Right here." Cissy pointed to her scar.

The two officers nodded and smiled.

Missy made the rest of the introductions and then asked, "I assume nothing happened during the shower, right?"

"We really didn't think anything would happen but wanted to be prepared in case," Juanita assured

Missy. "They brought more cameras." She indicated the officers. "We'll be installing them now that your guests are gone."

"I'd forgotten about the situation during the shower." Missy sighed. "Being with friends took my mind off things."

"It was a wonderful night for you, my dear." Mrs. Franklin put her arm around her future daughter-in-law's shoulders. "Focus on the friends who were here wishing you the best. You are loved, and God is with you."

"I know." Missy's eyes watered. "Sometimes the whole situation overwhelms me, and I have to remind myself God is in control."

"I should go. Everything's cleaned up. All the extra food is in the fridge." Mrs. Franklin kissed Missy on the cheek. "So, now go look at all your gifts and relax. Goodnight and sleep well."

"Thank you so very much for all you've done." Missy opened the front door.

"I'll go, too." Becky hugged her friend. "I'll see you tomorrow for the fitting."

"Yes, come over, and we'll drive to the dress shop together." Missy closed the door and turned to Juanita. "Is there anything I can do besides stay out of your way?"

"No, we'll get started installing the cameras." Juanita motioned to the others to follow her back upstairs.

Missy watched them and then went back into

the family room with her twin following.

"Boy, you sure have some generous friends." Cissy picked up a mixer.

"Yep, they are wonderful." Missy grinned.

* * *

Saturday morning, Missy stood in the family room with Cissy while looking over the gifts again. "I'm going to have a hand cramp after writing all the thank-you notes." She indicated the gifts around the room.

"I know." Cissy took a sip of her tea. "I'll help by writing the gift on the back of each card, so you can put them in your bridal shower book."

"I never thought about doing that." Missy sat down on the couch. "I thought I was going to have to keep each card with the package, so I'd know who gave me what."

"Mrs. Franklin wrote down the presents and who gave it as you opened them." Cissy set down her cup and picked up a box with towels in it.

"Really? I didn't know she was keeping track of all of them." Missy stood and walked over to the chair Mrs. Franklin sat in the night before. She found the list. "Here it is. This is great. I can write the notes from it. I guess we need to put all these gifts somewhere." Missy looked around the room.

Cissy put down the towels. "Where do you suggest?"

"We use the family room more than the living room. Let's get a folding table and put it in there so I can display them. When Ryan comes home, he'll want to see everything. For now, I'll take a picture and send it to him." Missy walked down the hall toward the living room.

"I'll get the table." Cissy followed her. "Is it in the garage?"

"Yes." Missy put a finger to her temple. "I think it's by the wall opposite the door."

"Okay." Cissy turned toward the garage door. "I'll be back in a minute."

Missy moved the end table closer to the couch to make room for the folding table. The sound of the phone ringing had Juanita running down the stairs as Missy picked it up.

"Hello." Missy turned towards Juanita when she heard her enter the room.

"This is Marshal Horton."

"Oh, hello, Marshal. Do you need to speak to Juanita?" Missy asked.

"No, I need to talk to you."

"Is something wrong?" She held the phone, so Juanita could hear also.

"I've been thinking about how your father would have given me the information," the marshal replied. "I think he had a thumb drive he was going to give me."

"A thumb drive? Do you think it may be here?"

"Yes, I do."

"I can look though my father's things," Missy said. "I don't know where he'd have kept it."

"Could it be with his personal items from the accident?"

"I don't remember seeing anything like that, but I can look."

"Good. If it's not there, could you look through his desk and anywhere else you think he might have hidden it?" the marshal asked.

"There wasn't anything with his computer when I got it for you," Missy reminded him. "I'll look around and let you know."

"Thanks. If you do find one, give it to Juanita and she can make sure it's what we're looking for."

"Okay, bye." Missy hung up the phone and turned to see Cissy standing in the doorway with the folding table.

"Put the table over by the wall." Missy pointed. "We'll put the gifts on it later. Right now, we have some searching to do."

"What's going on?" Cissy placed the table in the living room.

Missy moved past her sister and said over her shoulder, "It seems there may be a thumb drive in the house which Daddy intended to give to Marshal Horton."

"Where do you think it might be?" Cissy followed her twin and Juanita up the stairs.

"I don't know. I'll look in the bag from the hospital which has Daddy's things in it from the accident." Missy motioned to Juanita and Cissy to enter her parents' room. "Y'all look in his desk and closet."

"I'll look in the closet." Juanita looked at Cissy. "You look around the room. Be sure to look under everything."

"Okay." Cissy followed Juanita into the master bedroom.

Teresa looked up from the surveillance monitor. "What's going on?"

"We need to search this room for a thumb drive," Juanita told her.

"Where do you want me to look?" Teresa asked.

"You can look in the desk while you keep an eye on the monitors." Juanita motioned to Stephanie. "Help me look in the closet."

* * *

Missy entered her room and lifted the window seat where the bags of her parents' and brother's effects were. She picked up her father's bag and a tear fell down her cheek. "I miss you so much, Daddy," Missy mumbled. She took all the bags and went into her parents' room.

"Juanita, here are the things from the hospital." Missy set them on the bed.

"Did you look in them for the thumb drive?" Juanita asked as she came out of the closet.

"No, I'm . . . I'm sorry, I just can't." Missy's voice

was thick with tears.

"Oh, Missy." Cissy pulled her into a hug. "It's okay. You don't have to look through their things. We can do it."

"I'm sorry." Missy sniffled.

"Don't be." Cissy rubbed her sister's back. "You have nothing to be sorry about. It's normal for you to be upset."

Juanita sat down on the bed and picked one up. "I'll look through the bags."

"Thank you." Missy wiped the tears from her cheek. "I know they're just things, but the memory of them gives me an ache in my heart."

"It's going to take time, but eventually the good memories will come to mind when you think of them and not just the loss." Juanita looked at the bag she was holding. "Are these your dad's or your brother's things?"

"It's Daddy's things."

"Let's empty it." Juanita dumped everything out of the bag onto the bed. "There's not one here."

"Should we look in the others?" Cissy picked up another one.

"Yes, just in case their things became mixed up." Juanita replaced everything in the bag she was holding. "Give me another, please."

"Here's Mrs. Calhoun's. It has a purse in it." Cissy handed it to Juanita.

Juanita emptied the contents and picked up the purse. "May I open the purse, Missy?"

Missy nodded. "I don't think Daddy would've given it to Momma to keep."

"Just in case, I need to look." Juanita went through it then returned the purse inside the pouch. "Nope, not in it. Give me the last one."

"This has my brother's things." Missy handed the bag to Juanita.

"Okay. Let's see what's in here." Juanita dumped everything on the bed. "Don't see any thumb drive here, either."

Stephanie came out of the closet. "Hey, I found one."

"Good. Hopefully it's what we need." Juanita took it from Stephanie and handed it to Teresa. "Put this in the laptop and pull up what's on it."

"Okay." Teresa plugged it into the computer. "I don't think this is what you're looking for. It has a list of things to do."

Missy moved behind Teresa. "It looks like Momma's file on the wedding."

Juanita motioned for Teresa to stand up, and she took the seat. "Let me open all the files to make sure, but I think you're right."

"Do you want us to keep searching?" Stephanie asked.

Juanita nodded while scrolling through the files. "Yes. This isn't the one we want." She took the thumb drive and handed it to Missy. "You'll want this."

"Thanks." Missy smiled and held it close to her heart.

"We need to keep looking." Juanita stood. "Teresa, continue watching the monitors."

"Okay." Teresa sat down at the desk.

"Where do you want me to check?" Missy asked.

"Is there any place in the house your father spent a lot of time?" Juanita pushed her hair behind her ear.

"He has . . . had a workshop in the garage," Missy replied.

"Go look in every drawer, in and around everything." Juanita turned to Stephanie. "Go with her. She shouldn't be out there by herself."

Stephanie nodded and followed Missy.

* * *

"The workshop takes up half of the garage. We can only get one car inside." She opened the inside door to the garage and turned on the light.

"Missy, you start at this end of the worktable; I'll start at the other end." Stephanie walked to the front of the garage by the closed doors.

"I have some good memories of Daddy working out here." Missy sighed. "He'd be here for hours, but I never knew what he was doing."

"He has arranged everything neatly." Stephanie pulled out a drawer.

"Yes." Missy opened a cabinet. "He always told me, 'There's a place for everything and everything has its place.' I was the messy one."

"I can see he lived by the saying." Stephanie closed the drawer and opened another one.

"Do you know why Marshal Horton can't get the information from the bank?" Missy asked.

"The only thing I can think of is your dad must've obtained information not in the bank records." Stephanie opened the last drawer.

"I wonder what it could be," Missy mused. "Can you tell me anything about the case?"

"Sorry, no." Stephanie closed the drawer. "I'm not privy to all the information, but I do know the suspect's not at the top of the chain, so to speak. Maybe your dad had something leading to someone else."

"This is so new and scary to me." Missy looked behind some boards. "I've never dreamed someone would use our bank to do something illegal."

"The problem with money laundering is, it's hard to catch someone doing it if they have smarts about it." Stephanie kneeled to run her hand under the table. "Most crooks use other methods and don't take the risk of using banks."

"I don't know anything about it. What's the reason?" Missy picked up a tool box and opened the lid.

"When a drug dealer gets money, most times it's in small bills. They need to either get larger bills or have a place to keep the money." Stephanie stood. "You'd be surprised the amount of money we confiscate during a drug bust."

"It's just . . . well, I guess I'm so naïve about

what's happening in our town." Missy pulled tools out of the box. "I tend to think the best of everyone."

"I don't have the privilege of thinking that way. Most of the people I encounter are not on the right side of the law." Stephanie looked around the garage and pointed toward some shelves. "I didn't find anything here. I think I'll look in those boxes."

"All the boxes are labeled." Missy put the tools back in the tool box. "Most of them are decorations for Christmas, Thanksgiving, and other holidays. Momma always loved to decorate."

Missy and Stephanie worked in silence while looking in boxes, behind, and under shelves.

Stephanie looked at Missy. "How are you holding up with all you've been through?"

"It's hard," Missy replied. "I've had one thing after another happen. Sometimes when I'm alone, I think it's all a dream. Then I hear Juanita or Cissy and know it's real."

"I'm sorry." Stephanie looked at Missy. "You're a strong person."

"No." Missy smiled. "It's God's strength upholding me and giving me the courage to go on every day."

"Do you blame God for the death of your family?" Stephanie asked.

Missy shook her head. "God didn't cause the accident."

"God could've stopped it."

"I see now how God used this tragedy to bring

a good thing into my life," Missy replied. "I do know God sees the whole picture, and I don't. I believe He's helping me through all of this and will continue to do so. One of the pros in the situation so far is finding sisters I didn't know I had."

"Juanita told us about your reunion with them." Stephanie replaced another box after looking through it. "How did it feel to find out you were adopted?"

"I was shocked." Missy took another container off the shelf. "I couldn't understand why my parents didn't tell me. I still don't."

"You weren't mad?" Stephanie reached for another tote.

"You know . . ." Missy looked at Stephanie. "I'm not mad. I'm confused. I don't know why they didn't tell me. I understand their lawyer knew all along and encouraged them to tell me. I'm going to talk to him as soon as I can to see if he can tell me why."

"I hope you find out." Stephanie put the last box back on the shelf. "Well, I don't think he hid it in here. Can you think of any other place he would hide things?"

"No, I never could find where he hid my Christmas presents." Missy smiled and walked toward the door to the house. "He could be secretive."

"Is there any place in the house your dad might think no one would look?" Stephanie followed Missy. "Maybe in your brother's room or yours?"

Missy hesitated for a second and then smiled. "Yes, I have a compartment in my window seat. When

I was little, I kept my special treasures in it. Let's look there." She hurried up the stairs with Stephanie right behind her. "I haven't looked in it for years." Walking into her room and over to the window seat, she lifted the lid.

Stephanie looked inside. "I don't see any compartment."

"You won't see it because it's hidden." Missy reached down and placed her thumb over a knot hole and pushed. The bottom popped up. She lifted it out and revealed a box beneath it. "I don't remember this being here." She took the box out and opened it. Inside lay a thumb drive and a note under it.

Stephanie took the drive while Missy opened the note and started reading. "What does it say?"

Missy looked at her and cleared her throat. "My dearest Missy, I have hidden this box with the thumb drive in your secret place, because it is very important it gets to Marshal Horton. His number is on the card in the bottom of the box. If you found this, and I am still around, I'll take it to him. But, if something has happened to me, I'm so sorry." Tears escaped Missy's eyes and she grabbed a tissue before continuing. "I know what I'm doing can be dangerous and cause our family a great deal of sorrow. There are so many things I should have told you but kept putting them off. I hope I'll be able to tell you in person, but if not, your mother will explain everything. I'm so sorry if I can't be there for you. Know I love you very much, and you're a special young lady. Love, Daddy." Missy sobbed as she leaned against the window seat with the note shaking in her hands.

"I'll take the thumb drive to Juanita." Stephanie touched Missy's shoulder.

"Okay." Missy sniffed and looked up at Stephanie. "I want to sit here for a moment."

A few minutes later Cissy entered her twin's bedroom. "Missy?"

"Daddy left me this." She handed the note to her sister.

Cissy read it and knelt beside Missy.

"I guess he was going to tell me about being adopted." She blew her nose.

"I think so, too." Cissy handed the note back to her.

"I still wonder why he never told me." She looked at his familiar script again.

Juanita walked into the room. "I think this is what the marshal needs. I'll give him a call." She turned and left.

Cissy took her sister's hand and squeezed it. "I don't know what you're thinking, but I do know God gave you a good life with your family. Now He's given you sisters, so we can help you through this situation. His timing is never ours, because He can see everything, and He knew you'd need us at this time in your life."

Missy nodded. "I know God has my best interest, but it still hurts losing someone you love. I lost three people who were a big part of my life. Cissy, I am so glad you're here with me." She started crying again.

Juanita returned. "Excuse me, Marshal Horton is on his way."

The twins hugged with relief. The danger was nearly over.

* * *

The marshal received the thumb drive from Juanita. "I'll take this to my office and if it's what we need, we should have Delgado arrested very soon."

"Is that his name?" Missy asked. "Will I have to do anything else?"

"Please keep his name to yourself. Since you had no knowledge of what's going on, I don't think you'll be involved any further."

"That's a relief." Missy sighed.

"I do want Juanita and the other officers to stay here with you until he's behind bars," Marshal Horton said. "It's only a precautionary measure. The danger to you will be over soon. There shouldn't be any other attempts to break-in once he's in custody."

Missy smiled. "I'll be very happy to get my life back or should I say, start my new life."

"I'll keep in touch and let you know what I can in regard to what's happening." The marshal extended his hand toward Missy.

Missy shook his hand. "Ok, Marshal Horton. I'd appreciate it."

Chapter 13

Promptly at twelve thirty, the group left the house for their dress fitting at the bridal shop.

"Tell me where we're going," Juanita stated as she opened the driver's door.

"It's the Taylor Bridal Boutique on Kemp Boulevard across from Sikes Senter." Missy opened the passenger door and got in the front seat as Becky and Cissy entered in the backseat.

"I'm so excited to see your dress, Missy." Cissy giggled.

"I forgot you haven't seen my gown. It's simple but beautiful." Tears came to Missy's eyes as she continued. "Momma helped me pick it out. I wish she were here."

Becky patted her shoulder from the back seat. "I know this will be difficult for you, but remember the joy your mom had while helping you choose the perfect one."

"Thanks, Becky." Missy turned her head and gave a small smile. "Momma's excitement matched mine when we looked at all the gowns and agreed on the one I chose."

"Your mom always wanted the best for you." Becky leaned back in the seat and said to Cissy, "She had the best fashion sense and was always so organized."

"I wish you could've met her," Missy stated. "She was a wonderful mother and so supportive. Momma always led me to God's Word when I was confused about something."

"She sounds somewhat like my mom." Cissy looked out the car window. "She always has the right verse for me when I need direction."

"Yes, Momma did the same thing." Missy looked back at Cissy. "Do you think they were twins?" Missy giggled.

"Funny." Cissy laughed. "God gave us moms who know Him and raised us to be daughters of the King."

"True." Missy played with her purse straps. "I have to remember all the things she taught me and fully rely on God."

Juanita parked as close to the door as possible. "Let's get inside quickly and please, stay together."

Everyone exited the car and walked to the bridal shop door. Juanita looked around the area to make sure no one followed them.

Mrs. Taylor, the owner, greeted them as they entered the shop. "Missy, it's good to see you. Are you ready to try on your gown?"

"Hello, Mrs. Taylor." Missy nodded to the others.

"We're all excited to see my gown and their dresses. I'd like you to meet Juanita. She's visiting me for a while."

Mrs. Taylor nodded toward Juanita and then touched Missy's arm. "Missy, my dear, I'm so sorry about your loss. I heard it on the news and when Cissy came into the shop to get a dress, I was confused until she told me she was your twin sister. She explained things to me."

"Thank you." Missy smiled. "It was a surprise when I first met her, a little confusing, but delightful."

"It's an interesting story. I can hardly believe everything that's happened to you. Finding your sisters when you needed them so much was a blessing. God has His little gifts to give just when you need them, doesn't He?" Mrs. Taylor smiled at Missy. "Now, you're here to get ready for a very joyous occasion." She took Missy's arm and guided her toward the hallway with the dressing rooms. "Your gown is in the first room. Becky, yours is in the second, and Cissy you're in the third room. Go change into the dresses, and if you need help, just call out and I'll come."

Juanita stayed near the front of the hallway in view of the first room where Missy changed.

Becky was the first one to come out in her gown. "Well, what do you think, Juanita?" She twirled around in her rosy pink-colored dress. A simple A-line with three-quarter length sleeves.

"It's beautiful," Juanita said. "I like the color."

"Missy's favorite color." Becky touched the roses on the sleeve of her left arm. "I love the delicate roses."

Cissy stepped out of her dressing room and walked up to Becky and Juanita. "How do I look?"

"Beautiful." They said at the same time and both looked at each other.

"Is this how it feels when you and Missy say the same thing at the same time?" Juanita asked.

"I suppose so, but there's always a tingle up my spine when she says what I'm thinking." Cissy grinned. "I love this dress."

"I do, too," Becky replied. "Yours fits nicely. I don't think you'll need anything else done with it, do you?"

"No, it feels wonderful." Cissy smoothed the skirt of the dress. "It fit well when I first tried it on, but Mrs. Taylor said it needed a tuck here and there."

"Turn around," Mrs. Taylor said as she approached them from the back room.

Cissy and Becky both turned at the same time. They both chuckled.

"I feel pretty, oh so pretty," Cissy sang.

"You both are very pretty in your gowns," Mrs. Taylor said. "Let me have a look at each of you to see if anything else needs to be taken in."

"Could someone come help me?" Missy called out. "I'm having trouble with my gown."

"I'm coming," Mrs. Taylor replied as she walked to the dressing room and opened the door. "I figured you would need some help with the buttons."

"I can't get all of them." Missy turned so Mrs. Taylor could see the back of the gown.

"No problem, you've almost got it." She finished the last of the buttons. "How does it feel?"

"It feels perfect." Missy looked in the mirror on the wall and asked, "How does it look?"

"Walk out front so I can see it with more light." Mrs. Taylor opened the door and announced, "Here she comes."

Everyone turned and watched as Missy exited the dressing room and walked up the hallway toward them.

"Wow," Cissy exclaimed. "You're beautiful."

"So are you." Missy grinned. "The color is perfect on you both."

Mrs. Taylor guided Missy over to the full-length mirrors and onto the little platform. The others followed. Juanita went and stood by the front window.

"Turn around, so I can see it from all sides." Mrs. Taylor said.

Missy turned slowly so the flowing skirt moved with her. "I love it."

"The bodice fits well, and the skirt flows the way it's supposed to." Mrs. Taylor waved for Missy to continue turning. "Does it feel too tight or too loose anywhere?"

"I think it's a perfect fit," Missy said, grinning. "I feel so wonderful."

"I believe it's perfect, too." Mrs. Taylor stepped on the platform and ran her hands down the back. "There are so many buttons, but they lie nicely." She looked at the other ladies. "What do you think, ladies?"

"I agree with Cissy. Wow!" Becky smiled. "I love the roses on my sleeves. I see the roses are also on your bodice." She pointed to Missy's gown.

"Momma wanted the dresses to have something to connect with my gown." Missy smiled and turned to look at herself in the mirror. "The little roses were her idea. Can I also try on the veil and train?"

"Yes, let me get them for you." Mrs. Taylor stepped off the platform. "Be back in a minute. By the way, do you have your shoes with you, so I can see if the dress length is right?"

"Yes, all of our shoes are in the trunk of the car." Missy turned to Juanita. "We forgot to bring them in when we arrived."

"I'll get them. Everyone stays inside," Juanita said.

She left the shop and returned in a few minutes with three boxes. "Here you go ladies." Juanita stepped back to the front of the store looking out the window.

Becky took a box and opened it. "These are Missy's." She took the shoes out and placed them on the platform, so Missy could step into them.

Cissy held up a pair of shoes. "I think these are mine." She put them on the floor and stepped into them. "Yes, they're mine."

Becky picked up the last box, removed the shoes, and put them on. "I'm so glad you said we didn't have to wear high heels. These flats are nice."

"I agree." Cissy nodded. "I don't wear heels very often. They kill my feet and since we'll be standing, these will be more comfortable."

"You're welcome." Missy replied. "I don't like heels either. When I saw those shoes, I knew they were perfect. They're simple but dressy enough for the wedding. My shoes have just a little heel but not too high to hurt my feet."

"Here we go." Mrs. Taylor walked toward Missy holding the train over her arm. "Becky, will you hold the veil while I attach the train?"

"I'd be happy too." Becky took the veil and looked at the detail on it. "There are tiny roses on the veil, too. It's so beautiful, Missy."

"I know." Missy nodded. "Momma picked out the fabric to match the roses on our dresses."

"Your mom had a good eye for coordinating things." Mrs. Taylor buttoned the train to the back of Missy's gown. "Did you know I asked her to think about working here with me?"

"No." Missy looked at Mrs. Taylor by way of the mirror. "She didn't say anything to me about it."

"Well, she told me she'd think about it but if she decided to, it would be after your wedding." Mrs. Taylor glanced at Missy in the mirror. "She wanted to spend as much time with you as she could until your wedding. She loved you very much."

Tears trickled down Missy's cheek. "I loved her so much and miss her right now."

"Hey." Mrs. Taylor pulled tissues from the box on the side table and handed them to Missy. "I didn't mean to make you cry. I just thought you'd like to know how much she cared about you."

"I'm sorry." Missy dabbed her eyes. "Sometimes the tears start, and I can't stop them."

"I understand." Mrs. Taylor gave Missy a little hug. "I've lost someone I loved quite suddenly, too, and I still get teary eyed thinking about them. It'll get easier and with God's help you'll get through this time of grief. It'll take time. Don't think you have to stop crying when the grief hits. Let it out, but please be careful with this gown on."

"I'm sorry." Missy wiped her eyes again. "I didn't get any tears on it, did I?"

"No, it's okay." Mrs. Taylor stepped off the platform. "Turn so I can see how the train looks."

"Put her veil on so we can see it all together." Becky handed the veil to Mrs. Taylor.

"Will you have your hair up or down?" Mrs. Taylor asked as she set the veil on Missy's head.

"Ryan likes my hair down," Missy said. "It'll be down but with the sides gathered to the top and curls down the back."

"Good." Mrs. Taylor straightened the veil and looked at Missy. "The veil will fit fine with what you've described."

"Oh, Missy." Cissy smiled. "You're beautiful even with the runny mascara."

"Everything will be perfect on your wedding day," Becky chimed in. "Ryan won't be able to take his eyes off you as you walk down the aisle."

"Well, then." Mrs. Taylor took the veil from

Missy's head and handed it back to Becky. "I think it's unanimous; you'll be a beautiful bride. Time to look at the bridesmaids and their dresses."

Missy carefully stepped off the platform and turned to Becky. "Your turn."

Becky handed the veil back to Mrs. Taylor, stepped on the platform, and faced the mirror. "I like it. What do you think, Mrs. Taylor?"

"Yes, it fits great. Is there any place where it seems to be too tight?" Mrs. Taylor asked while looking at the dress.

"No." Becky did a little turn to see the back. "I'm glad I don't have all the buttons on the back like Missy does." She turned to her friend. "I'll be there to help with your buttons."

"Thanks." Missy smiled. "I knew I could count on you."

"Okay, Cissy, it's your turn," Mrs. Taylor said.

Becky stepped off the platform and Cissy stepped on it.

"I'm so giddy." Cissy chuckled. "I've never been in a wedding before, and in the next four months I'll be in two."

"Two?" Mrs. Taylor asked.

"Yes, my . . . our sister, Gayle, is getting married in a couple of weeks." Cissy looked at the group. "I'm maid of honor in her wedding."

"Gayle asked me to light the family candle," Missy told everyone. "It was too late to add me as a bridesmaid. I'm a little nervous about our first big event as a family."

Cissy stepped down from the platform and took her twin's hands. "I know sometimes it feels awkward, but you'll get used to it. It took me a while, but now I feel at ease with our sisters."

"Well, ladies, I think we're through here." Mrs. Taylor placed the veil across a chair, so she could remove the train from Missy's gown. "Just tell your other sisters to come in for their fittings. Their dresses are ready, too. Please be careful when you take off the dresses. Place the hangers on the dressing room hook, and I'll put them in the bags for safe keeping. I'll deliver them to your house the day before the wedding."

"Thank you so very much, Mrs. Taylor," Missy said. "You've done everything my mom wanted."

After changing out of the gowns, the group returned to the car. Juanita started the engine but didn't back out of the parking lot.

"Is something wrong?" Missy asked.

"There's been a car driving up and down the street. I noticed it when I got your shoes out of the trunk. It's just now coming down the street again."

All eyes moved toward the direction Juanita looked. They watched the car pull along the curb and stop.

"We'll sit here a few minutes to see what's going on." Juanita pulled her cell phone out and called the chief. "Sir, could you check on a gray Ford SUV with license number MMS451. It's been circling the block where we are located. Don't want to move until it's clear."

Everyone kept watch on the car and didn't know they were holding their breath until they heard Juanita exhale. "Thanks, Chief." She replaced her phone in her pocket. "False alarm. Not our suspect."

A few moments later an elderly woman came out of the store next to the bridal shop, carrying bags, opened the door of the SUV and got in.

"Is this how it's going to feel every time a suspicious vehicle drives by?" Missy choked out.

"I didn't want to disturb your fitting, so I kept an eye on the SUV, but couldn't get a clear plate number to check it out until now. Sorry to scare you. I'd rather play it safe than to cause a commotion."

Juanita backed out of the parking spot and drove them back to the safety of Missy's home.

Chapter 14

Stephanie threw off the covers, slid her legs over the side of the bed, and glanced at Teresa. "How's everything looking?"

"All's quiet, but Missy just went downstairs." Teresa clicked the keyboard to bring up the image of Missy in the kitchen.

"She's up early." Stephanie stood and stretched. "I wonder if she's okay."

"When you get breakfast why don't you ask her?" Teresa picked up her glass of water and took a sip.

"Okay. Let me change clothes." Stephanie walked into the bathroom. "Did Missy look upset?"

"No, actually, she seemed to be smiling."

Stephanie stuck her head out of the bathroom door. "Smiling? At this time in the morning?"

"Yes, it's kind of strange. She's usually the last one up."

Stephanie changed into jeans and T-shirt, then walked back into the bedroom, pulling her hair in a ponytail. "I'll get breakfast and check on her. Do you want me to bring you anything?"

"No, I'm fine. As soon as you get back, I'll take a shower and hit the hay."

"I'll be back soon." Stephanie left the room and went downstairs. As she entered the hallway, she headed toward the kitchen light.

Missy stood by the stove waiting for the water to boil, holding a cup with a tea bag. She was humming.

"Missy?"

Missy jumped, almost dropping the cup. She placed her hand over her heart as she turned toward the door. "Stephanie, you scared me."

"Sorry, didn't mean to. You're never up this early. Are you okay?"

"Yes, I'm okay, lost in my thoughts and didn't hear you. I'm making tea. Do you want some?"

"No, thanks. I'll make some coffee. So, what's the song you were humming?"

"Amazing Grace. It's one of my favorite songs. It calms me and helps me prepare for the day."

"I understand. This would be stressful by itself let alone what you've been though." Stephanie pulled the coffee from the cabinet and started making a pot. "So, why are you up so early?"

"After I went to bed last night, it occurred to me, I haven't had my quiet time since the day of the accident." Missy poured hot water from the teapot into the cup. "I decided I'd get up early this morning and get back in the routine."

"Quiet time?"

Missy searched Stephanie's face. "Quiet time is when I study God's Word, listen to what He has to say to me in the scriptures, and pray."

"Oh." Stephanie took a cup from the cabinet and spooned sugar into it.

"Stephanie, what do you know about Jesus?"

"Uh . . . well . . . Jesus was born on Christmas and died on a cross around Easter."

Missy nodded. "Would you mind coming to the family room while you're waiting for the coffee to brew. I want to tell you who Jesus is."

Stephanie followed Missy and they sat on the couch. "I'm not religious and I haven't been to church for many years," Stephanie said. "My mom took me when I was little but when she died . . . well, Dad didn't take me because he blamed God for not healing her."

"Stephanie, I'm so sorry. When did your mom die?"

"At the age of six. Dad was a good father. He worked hard. I didn't go without except the love of a mother. He said no other woman could hold a candle to Mom, so he never remarried."

"You've heard stories about Jesus." Missy smiled. "Do you remember anything else besides what you've already said about Him?"

"I remember attending Sunday school and singing songs about Jesus, but I was so young."

"Jesus is God's Son. He came to earth as a human, so He could take the sins of the world on His shoulders. He died on the cross for you and for me."

Missy took her Bible off the coffee table and recited John 3:16 as she turned to the scripture. "For God so loved the world, He gave His only begotten Son, that whosoever believeth in Him should not perish, but have everlasting life."

"I remember that verse. Don't know exactly what it means."

"It means God loves us so much, He gave Jesus to be the final sacrifice for our sins. In Romans it says, 'All have sinned and fall short of the glory of God.'"

Stephanie nodded. "I know I've sinned. So, what does it mean 'fall short of the glory of God?'"

"It means you won't go to heaven except by believing in Jesus Christ. He's the way. I know without a doubt my parents and brother are in heaven with God because they asked Jesus to be their Lord, as I have done."

Stephanie reached for Missy's Bible.

Missy pointed to the verse as she set the Bible into her hands. "Jesus is here with us. If you want His forgiveness, all you have to do is ask."

"Ask?" Stephanie looked from the Bible to Missy's eyes. "This is so new to me. I don't even know what I'm feeling." Stephanie looked at her watch. "I've got to get back upstairs so Teresa can get some sleep."

"When you're ready, Jesus is waiting. I'm here to help. It's an easy step. You just have to take it."

Stephanie stood and handed the Bible back to Missy. "I'll think about what you've said."

Missy watched as Stephanie left the room and

heard her at the coffee pot and refrigerator. Missy knelt and prayed. "Dear Lord, You are so wonderful and loving. Help me show Your love to Stephanie as she is searching for meaning in her life even if she doesn't know it yet. I now understand her questioning me about why I'm not mad at You. Help me to say the right words to help her on her way to a saving grace."

She reached for the Bible and continued. *I've missed spending time in the Word. Please forgive me. I know You've been by my side all this time. Be with me today as I go to church to worship. It'll be strange with my parents and brother gone. Lord, thank you for giving me my sisters so I'll have family around me. Thanks for Cissy. What a wonderful blessing she is to me as well as my other sisters. Bless them, Lord. Give us time to get to know each other better and become a real family again. Be with Ryan while he's away from me. Keep him safe. Thank you, Lord, for giving him to me. I pray all these things in Jesus Christ's name. Amen.*

Missy rose and sat in the chair. She opened her Bible to Ephesians and starting reading.

* * *

Several hours later, Cissy found Missy reading the Bible. "How long have you been up?"

Missy looked up from the scriptures. "I've been awake since around five. I haven't had a quiet time with my Lord for two weeks, and I thought it was time to start again."

Cissy walked over to the couch and sat down. "I

know what you mean. I've had a few quiet times but not on a regular basis. If you feel like I do, having time with the Lord helps you to center your thoughts on Jesus all day long. When I don't have it, I feel empty."

"Yes, I'm out of sorts. I know He's with me but not getting to read the Word and praying every morning makes me feel I'm missing something."

"Yeah, I know we're going to church this morning and will hear God's Word but having time alone with Him gives me peace."

Missy closed her Bible and placed it on the coffee table. "It does the same for me, too. I hadn't realized how long I've been sitting here reading the scriptures. I guess I'm trying to make up for the days I've missed. We need to get breakfast and then ready for church."

Cissy rose from the couch. "Is Juanita going with us? I think she's Catholic. Will she want to go to her church?"

"I don't know. I guess I'll have to ask her. I had an interesting conversation with Stephanie this morning. Pray for her; she's confused about God."

"I guess I don't know much about Stephanie or Teresa. Juanita, either, for that matter. I've been so absorbed in this situation, I never thought about them."

"I know. I had a long talk with God this morning about being bolder to ask how others feel about Him. Stephanie talked about herself a little to me this morning, but I think she has been hurt emotionally in the past and needs someone to talk to. I prayed God will use me in this situation to bring her to a saving knowledge of Christ. I'll give God the glory and praise for the outcome. I want to be a witness on how He can use a difficult situation to His glory. I hope an opportunity will arise, so I can show her. I know our time with Stephanie being here is getting shorter. I pray God will give me another opportunity to talk with her."

"You're an inspiration to me." Cissy hugged her sister. "You have a great strength within you."

"Not my strength but God's." Missy wiped her cheeks as tears flowed.

"Hey, I didn't mean to make you cry." Cissy grabbed a tissue and handed it to her twin. "I only meant, you're an example of the humble person I'd like to be. I'm so blessed to have you as my sister."

"Thank you." Missy wiped her eyes. "The verse I'm leaning on to help me is Philippians 4:13 – 'I can do all things through Christ who strengthens me.' I don't know how people go through things like this without God."

"I know. I'm so thankful for His love." Cissy turned toward the kitchen. "We need to get breakfast, or we'll be very hungry by the end of church."

Juanita looked up as they entered the kitchen. She finished pouring a cup of coffee. "So, what's on the agenda for today?"

"Church," the twins answered together and giggled.

Juanita shook her head. "What church do you go to?"

"I go to the Highland Baptist Church, a few blocks from here," Missy replied.

"I usually attend Trinity Baptist Church, but I'm going with Missy today." Cissy took a cup from the cabinet and poured coffee.

"What time does church start?" Juanita looked at her watch.

"Eleven." Missy poured hot water into her cup. "I'm not going to Sunday school today. I usually teach a youth class, and they'll have all kinds of questions as to why I haven't been there. I'm not in the frame of mind to teach yet. I've already told my co-leader, and she's covering for me again. Besides, there'll be enough questions from the adults, and it'll be hard to answer them."

Juanita took a sip of coffee. "You can't tell people what's going on, and I don't want you to feel uncomfortable trying to come up with answers."

"Okay, we have a little longer than I thought since it's only eight." Cissy opened the refrigerator and removed a carton of eggs. "I want an omelet this morning. How about y'all?"

"Sounds good to me," Juanita said. "I'm going to check in with Teresa and Stephanie. They may also want something to eat." Juanita left the kitchen and headed upstairs.

"Missy, if you would chop up the ham, onions, and bell pepper, I'll make western omelets." Cissy took

the pan from the cabinet and put it on the stove.
"Okay, chef." Missy grinned.

Chapter 15

Missy, Cissy, and Juanita entered the church and took a seat near the back. Missy wasn't ready to sit in her family's usual spot. They got a lot of stares and confusing looks because not many knew about Cissy. Missy greeted each one as they stopped by to give condolences, and she introduced them to her twin and Juanita.

"Missy, I'm so glad to see you here today." Pastor Kevin gave her a hug.

"Thanks, Pastor. You remember Cissy from the funeral, and this is my friend, Juanita." Missy nodded to them.

"Glad to see you again, Cissy. I still do a double take when I see you two together." Pastor Kevin shook her hand and turned to Juanita. "It's very nice to meet you. Are you just visiting, or do you live in the area?"

Juanita shook his hand. "I'm visiting Missy for a little while."

"Good, right now she needs to have people around her." The pastor looked at Missy. "Are you doing okay?"

"I'm adjusting," she replied. "I'm trying to get back into some kind of a routine."

"Let me know if you need to talk or anything else." Pastor Kevin looked at his watch. "Sorry, must get up front. It's time to start the service. Hope y'all will enjoy being here." He turned and walked down the aisle.

Missy breathed a sigh of relief when the service started. She was already weary from explaining Cissy to everyone. She simply wanted to worship and take her mind off the events of the past two weeks. She was deep in thought when everyone stood to sing the first song. Song after song brought peace. She felt God's presence and protection. When the service ended, others rushed to greet Missy and ask questions before she could leave her seat.

"Let's go out the side door," Juanita whispered to Missy.

Missy nodded. "Thank you, Mrs. Jennings, for your comforting words. I should go now as my friends need to leave. See you next week." Missy turned and followed Juanita and Cissy out of the church.

* * *

Once in the car, Juanita said, "You have a lot of friends, Missy."

"More like acquaintances and friends of my parents. Thanks for helping me end the conversation with Mrs. Jennings. She's a talker and was going on and on about the deaths she's had in her life."

"I saw how uneasy you looked and wanted to get you out of there." Juanita started the car. "Where to now, ladies?"

"Do you want to go out to eat or should we go back to the house and eat leftovers?" Missy put her seat belt on and turned to Cissy in the backseat. "Are you tired of leftovers?"

"Yeah, I'm in the mood for a juicy steak. I know a good place not too far from here." Cissy licked her lips. "I love their baked sweet potato with cinnamon butter."

"Steak it is." Juanita backed out of the parking space. "You'll have to give me directions."

"Okay." Cissy looked around and pointed left. "Turn left as you exit the parking lot. It's not far."

"Do you think I should call Stephanie and see if we can bring her something?" Missy asked. "I know Teresa is supposed to be sleeping."

"I'm sure she'd like to have a steak lunch." Juanita turned left as she told Missy the number to Stephanie's cell phone.

Stephanie picked up after the first ring. "Hello."

"Hey, Stephanie, it's Missy. We're going out for lunch and wanted to know if you want us to bring you something."

"Missy, I'm glad you called. Can I talk to Juanita?"

Missy held out the phone to Juanita. "She wants to talk to you."

Juanita pulled over to the curb and took the phone. "What's up?" She listened and started frowning. "Okay, we'll be there in a few minutes." Juanita handed the phone back to Missy. "Change of plans. We need to get back to the house."

"What's wrong?" Missy returned her phone to her purse.

"A car has driven by the house several times. It stopped at the curb about fifteen minutes ago. A man went to the door and rang the doorbell." Juanita pulled away from the curb. "Of course, no one answered, so he went back to his car and left. Stephanie wants us to look at the surveillance images to see if you know him."

"He didn't try to break-in, did he?" Missy asked.

"No, he left, but we have to check him out." Juanita continued driving and finally turned the corner onto Missy's street. "I don't see any strange cars, do you?"

Missy looked out the window. "No, I don't either. I recognize all the cars on the street."

Juanita pulled into the driveway. "Let's get into the house quickly."

They stepped out of the car and hurried to the door. Missy fumbled with the keys while trying to unlock the door. Finally, it opened, and they entered.

Juanita led the way up the stairs and entered Missy's parents' room. She looked at Stephanie. "We're here. Let's see the tape."

They stood behind Stephanie to watch the

monitor. She brought up the image of the man getting out of his car and walking to the door.

Juanita turned to Missy. "Do you recognize him?"

Missy smiled. "Yes, he's Richard Jameson." She turned to Cissy. "I think he came to see you."

"Me? Why would he come to see me. and how would he know I'm here?" Cissy asked. "He's *your* lawyer."

"On a Sunday? I don't think he's working today, so it must be a friendly visit." Missy nudged Cissy. "He likes you, and you like him. Admit it."

"Well . . . I . . . I do like him, but I didn't think anyone else knew it." Cissy beamed.

"Don't be silly. The few times he's been here, he's only had eyes for you." Missy turned and looked out the window. "I think he's coming back."

The doorbell rang. Cissy giggled nervously and started toward the door. "I'll answer it."

"Missy go down with her and don't let on about us." Juanita looked at the monitor again. "Nice-looking guy."

"Yep, and those two had sparks flying between them the moment they met." Missy exited the room and followed her twin downstairs.

Cissy opened the door. "Hi, Richard."

"Hi, Missy. Ah, no, you're Cissy, right?" Richard frowned.

"Yes, I am. Are you here to see my sister?" She turned her head toward Missy.

"No, well, actually I wanted to see you but didn't have your phone number, so I was going to ask Missy for it."

"Ask him to come in," Missy whispered in her twin's ear.

"Sorry, please come in." Cissy opened the door wider.

Richard entered. "Hello, Missy. I came by earlier, but no one answered, so I thought maybe you'd gone to church. I took a chance and came back by. I saw the car out front, so I stopped." He rubbed the back of his flushed neck. "Cissy, I was just wondering . . . well . . . would you like to have lunch with me? You haven't eaten, yet, have you? You're both invited."

"We were just talking about going to the steak house for lunch," Cissy replied and turned to Missy.

"Y'all go ahead." Missy grinned. "I think I'd like to have something simple. The leftovers in the fridge need to be eaten."

Richard smiled. "Are you sure? I'd like to get to know you both a little better."

"I'm sure." Missy turned toward the stairs. "Wait a minute. Cissy can you come upstairs with me for a minute?"

"Sure." She glanced at Richard. "Be right back." She followed her twin and Juanita met them in the hallway.

"Cissy just be careful while you're out with him," Juanita said quietly. "Be aware of your surroundings and anybody who may look like he's watching you. He doesn't know what's going on, does he?"

The sisters shook their heads. "I haven't told him anything," Missy replied. "I doubt he knows there was a break-in."

"I haven't seen him since the night of the spa day," Cissy added.

"Stay around people and don't go off by yourselves. If he suggests going someplace to be alone, make some excuse about having to get back here." Juanita shook her head. "I'm only trying to keep you safe while I'm not with you."

"I understand," Cissy sighed. "I'll come back here after we eat." She started downstairs and looked over her shoulder. "Be back soon."

Missy smiled as her twin walked down the stairs and heard her greet Richard as they left the house. She turned to Juanita. "You don't think she'll be in danger, do you?"

"Not if she does what I told her," Juanita assured her. "Let's go see what we can find to eat. Steak really did sound good."

* * *

Missy sat in the family room reading when she heard the front door open.

Cissy yelled, "We're back."

As the couple entered the family room, Missy laid her book down. "So, I see. Did you have a good lunch?"

"We did, and we brought you a piece of pie." Cissy handed a bag to her.

"Thank you." Missy took the container out of the bag. "Lemon Meringue, my favorite."

"We wanted to bring you something since you were having leftovers," Richard said looking at Cissy.

"Yeah, I felt a little guilty having steak and knowing what you were eating." Cissy shrugged.

"You're so kind." Missy stood. "I'm getting a fork." She walked toward the kitchen with the pie container in her hand.

Cissy watched her sister as she left the room then turned to Richard. "Can you stay for a little bit?"

"I can, but not long." Richard walked over to the couch and motioned for Cissy to sit first. "I have a new puppy at home and need to let her out soon."

"Aw, what kind is she?" Cissy asked as she sat on the couch.

"She's a Husky. Black and white with the bluest eyes."

Missy walked back into the family room eating the pie. "Yummy. This is so good."

"Glad you're enjoying it." Cissy smiled. "Richard was telling me he has a new puppy."

"Do you have a picture?" Missy returned to her chair.

"Yes, I do." Richard took out his phone and pulled up the picture and handed it to Cissy.

"She's so cute." She showed the picture to her twin.

"What's her name?" Missy asked.

"Well, I'm still trying to decide on a name. Right now, I'm calling her girl."

"She needs a name." Cissy put her finger to her temple. "Let me see if I can help you find one."

"I can use the help. This is the first puppy I've ever had." Richard smiled. "I now live in an apartment which allows pets."

"I have it!" Cissy exclaimed. "What about Precious?"

"Well, I don't know." Richard frowned at Cissy. "I don't see myself calling her Precious. Too girly for me."

Cissy smiled. "Oh, right. I see your point. You need a name which suits you and the puppy."

Richard nodded. "I want to take her for runs and don't want to be calling a big dog something that doesn't fit her."

"Okay, let me think again." Cissy pursed her lips and scratched her head.

"You know, she won't give up until the puppy has a name." Missy took another bite of her pie.

"I just want to help." Cissy looked at Missy then looked at Richard.

"You could write down some names for me to review." Richard stood. "I can't guarantee I'll choose any of them, but I will consider them. I must get back home."

Cissy also stood. "I'm sorry. I didn't mean to take over naming your puppy." She smiled at him. "I'd just love to help."

"No problem. I really do need to go." Richard turned to Missy. "It's nice seeing you again. We didn't get to talk much but Cissy told me the reason she's here. I'm glad you have someone with you while waiting for Ryan to come home." He looked at Cissy. "I know she wants to get to know you better, too." Looking back at Missy. "If there's anything I can do for you, please let me know."

"Thanks, Richard. She is a great comfort, and we're learning a lot about each other." Missy extended her hand. "I'll be calling your office to talk to Mr. Sims about a few things. Hope to see you again, soon."

"I hope to see you and your sister again, too." Richard shook her hand and turned to Cissy. "Will you walk me to the door?"

"Of course, I will." Cissy rose from the couch and followed him down the hallway.

Missy heard them talking but didn't understand what they said. She smiled to herself. *Yep, there's something going on between them.*

Cissy returned to the family room after showing Richard out and flopped down on the couch. "Well, I really made a mess of that conversation."

"It wasn't all bad." Missy took the last bite of her pie.

"Not bad! It was terrible. I completely embarrassed myself trying to take over naming his puppy." Cissy sat up. "I don't know why it's so important for me to find a name for her."

"You wanted to have something to connect with him." Missy put the empty container on the coffee table. "Just do what he said. Make a list of names and give it to him. Let him choose. Remember to pick names which won't embarrass him."

Cissy chortled as she stood. "I'll get started. By the way, he's very nice, and I do like him a lot. He asked me to go on a date this Friday." Cissy's eyes twinkled. "I'm so excited."

"I'm happy for you. I told you, he likes you."

"I'm going upstairs so I can think." Cissy turned toward the hallway. "I did feel like I was lying to him by not telling him everything going on here."

"I know, I feel the same way when I'm talking to someone who doesn't know the situation." Missy picked up her book. "Don't worry about it. Hopefully, this will be over soon."

"Okay, I'll be in my room if you need me." Cissy walked toward the door.

"I'll be fine. Mrs. Marple and I have a mystery to solve." Missy opened her book to where she'd been reading. "By the way, you owe me a steak dinner."

Cissy kept on walking, but Missy heard her snickering.

Chapter 16

Missy continued with student teaching every day hoping to hear from the marshal. It wasn't easy trying to act normal, but on Thursday evening she received the call.

"Marshal Horton here. I have some good news."

Although a bit leery, Missy asked, "What's the good news?"

"We've reviewed all the information on the thumb drive, and it's enough to get a warrant for the suspect's arrest. I have the DA working on it, so it shouldn't be much longer until we have him in custody."

"Does this mean the danger is almost over?" Missy turned and waved to Cissy as she entered the family room.

"Yes, it does. The policewomen will stay with you until we have him behind bars. A little longer if he gets out on bail."

"He'll know you have all the information about him, right?" Missy sat on the couch. "I should be safe."

"He may think you know something, and

you could be a witness against him," the marshal answered. "Don't think about it right now. Keep acting as if things are normal until we nab him."

Missy sighed. "I'm ready to get my life back to normal." She looked at Cissy with tears in her eyes. "At this point, I really don't know what my normal is."

"I know this is difficult for you. Continue doing what you are doing until you hear back from me."

"Okay, thanks for letting me know." Missy ended the call, stood, and hugged Cissy. "It's almost over. The marshal said the DA is getting a warrant for the arrest."

"I'm so happy for you." Cissy stepped back and looked into Missy's eyes. "It's a relief knowing the danger is finally coming to an end."

Juanita entered the room smiling. "So, you heard the news. The chief just told me, and I was coming to tell you when I heard the phone rang."

"Yes, I spoke with the marshal. I feel a weight has been lifted from my shoulders." Missy moved her shoulders up and down.

"I don't want to put the burden back on you, but until the suspect's in jail, he's still a threat." Juanita looked between the twins. "He doesn't know if all the information has been found and may come looking."

"Boy, you are a party pooper." Cissy flopped on the couch. "I'm trying to look on the bright side."

"Sorry, but we still need to be on alert," Juanita told them.

"I know." Cissy looked at Juanita. "I want things

to settle down as much as Missy does."

"It's a nightmare on top of a nightmare for me." Missy picked up her cup of tea and sat on the couch. "I need to see beyond this issue, but I can't seem to."

"It'll be okay." Cissy sat up straight and moved beside her twin. "You need to continue to think about your wedding and getting things ready. It'll take your mind off all the ugly stuff."

"I know you're right." Missy put her cup on the coffee table. "But until then, I'm thankful Ryan's mother is taking care of the wedding details. I'm praying there won't be a need for a bodyguard and policewomen on my wedding day."

"Things will work out." Cissy took her sister's hand. "Scripture says, 'I know the plans I have for you, plans to prosper you and not to harm you, plans to give you hope and a future.' You have faith, and God will get you through this situation so your future with Ryan will start off as it should."

"Your wedding is little over three months away, correct?" Juanita asked.

"Yes," Missy replied zoning out as thoughts of Ryan sprang into her mind.

"If they arrest Delgado, and keep him in jail, there's no reason you'll have us around by then." Juanita sat on the chair. "I know this is hard on you, it'd be hard on anyone. You're a strong young lady with faith in God I don't see very often in my line of work. You are an encouragement to me. I've watched how you handle things and how you rely on God."

"Thank you, Juanita." Missy wiped a tear off her cheek. "I don't feel strong all the time. I know God is with me and will get me through this. I can only trust the Lord's timing and have patience."

Stephanie entered the family room. "Juanita, there's another car driving by the house that's gone by a couple of times. Y'all come see if you recognize it."

Everyone followed Stephanie upstairs to the monitors.

"See, there it goes again." Teresa pointed to the monitor.

"Do you know who the car belongs to?" Juanita asked as she lifted the blind on the window a fraction to look out.

"No, I don't know the car," Missy replied and looked at Cissy. "Do you recognize it?"

"No." Cissy bent down to get a closer look at the monitor. "I think it's a Lincoln SUV."

"You're right." Teresa clicked some keys on the keyboard. "I'm trying to get the license plate but haven't been able to, yet."

"Well, ladies, it looks like we're not going anywhere tonight." Juanita pulled her phone from her pocket. "I'll call the chief and have an unmarked patrol car come by the area and maybe he'll be able to get a license plate."

Juanita called the chief as she walked out into the hallway.

"How many times has it gone by?" Missy asked Teresa.

"I've counted four times." Teresa made an adjustment on the monitor trying to zoom in on the image. "I can't get the right angle to see the tag."

"Okay, I'm scared it may be Delgado." Missy looked at Cissy.

"I know. I'm scared, too." Cissy put her arm around her twin's shoulders.

"The chief will have an unmarked car come by in a few minutes," Juanita stated as she walked back into the room.

"Will they stop or just drive by?" Missy asked.

"They'll drive around the neighborhood, look for the car, and get the license number." Juanita put her phone back in her pocket. "I gave them the description and they'll keep tabs on it while finding out who it belongs to."

"What do we do now?" Missy asked.

"There's nothing you can do." Juanita nodded towards Teresa and Stephanie. "They'll keep an eye on the monitors and let us know if anything happens."

"Come on, Missy." Cissy turned her sister towards the door. "Let's go start supper. It'll take our mind off things."

"I'll do anything to stop thinking about what may happen." Missy followed her twin to the bedroom door and looked back to the policewomen. "We'll make grilled chicken and a salad. Sound okay to y'all?"

"Sounds good," Juanita replied. "I'll let you know when we find out who's driving the SUV."

"Okay." Missy coaxed a weary smile. "By the

way, I don't think I've said this before, but, thank you, ladies, for protecting me . . . us." Missy looked at her sister. "We really appreciate your dedication." She turned and left the room with Cissy following.

* * *

"Missy, you haven't eaten much." Cissy pointed to her plate.

"I guess I've lost my appetite." She laid her fork down. "After the marshal told me the news about the pending arrest, I felt relieved. Now, with the SUV driving around, I'm tense again."

"I know." Cissy took a bite of her salad. "It's one step forward and two steps back."

"When is this going to stop?" Missy sobbed and put her napkin to her eyes.

Cissy reached out and touched Missy's shoulder. "I know it's upsetting not knowing what will happen. I'm praying for God to intervene and get things settled for you."

"I'm sorry." Missy dabbed her eyes. "I've never cried so much in my whole life."

"You've a good reason to cry." Cissy stood and moved behind her sister and began massaging her shoulders. "As Juanita said, you are strong. You're in a situation where you don't have any control. It'd make anyone upset."

"You're such a good sister." Missy patted her twin's hand.

"Hey, I'm here for you. Come on, take a couple of bites."

"I'll try." Missy picked up her fork. "I wonder if they've found out whose SUV it is."

"Yes, we have." Juanita interjected as she walked into the dining room.

"Who?" the twins said at the same time.

Juanita walked over and sat in the chair beside Missy. "It's Delgado's."

"Oh," Missy exclaimed. "So, he does think there's something still here which can be used against him?"

"Yes, it looks like it." Juanita looked at the sisters. "We'll be watching the monitors all night. I don't think he'll break in while there's a car in the driveway. It's probably why he keeps driving by, hoping we'll leave."

"So, you think he'll break in when we leave tomorrow?" Missy asked.

"It's a possibility." Juanita stood. "The marshal is contacting the DA and letting him know the latest development, and maybe it will speed up issuing the warrant. By the way, the grilled chicken salad was very good." Juanita nodded toward Missy's plate. "It looks like you haven't eaten much."

"I'm not very hungry. My stomach's in knots right now." She stood, picked up her plate, and walked toward the kitchen. "I'll put it in the fridge for later, maybe."

"Juanita, she's really scared," Cissy whispered

as she stood. "I'm a little frightened, also."

"We're here to keep you safe." Juanita walked into the hallway. "I'll keep you informed."

"Okay, thanks." Cissy entered the kitchen where her twin stood by the refrigerator with her plate still in her hand. "Let me put it in a container so we can seal it." Cissy took the dish from her sister. "Good thing you didn't put salad dressing on it."

Missy looked at Cissy. "You never thought you'd be in this danger when you said you'd come and stay with me until Ryan comes home, did you?"

"No, it has been an adventure." She put the salad in a plastic container and snapped the lid on it. "Although we're getting to know each other in a way we never would have if not for this situation. I think we are going to be closer because of it."

"I wish it was a more normal situation," Missy sighed. "Like planning for my wedding and just waiting for Ryan to come home." She took the container and placed it in the refrigerator. "I'm glad you think of this as an adventure. I call it a nightmare."

Cissy took Missy's hands. "One day this nightmare will be over. You just need to stay strong until it is."

"I'm looking forward to that day." Missy embraced her twin. "I think I need to go write some 'thank you' notes. Maybe it'll help me get my mind off things."

"Good idea." Cissy stepped back and pushed a strand of hair out of Missy's eyes. "Do you need any help?"

"No, I'll be okay. If I can do at least ten notes, I can mail them out tomorrow." Missy headed to the family room.

"I'm going to get my book and I'll join you. Okay?"

"I'd like the company, thanks," Missy said.

* * *

Missy sat at the desk in the corner of the family room when Cissy returned with her book.

"I was just thinking." Missy clicked her pen. "If Delgado does try to break in while he thinks no one is home, Stephanie and Teresa will nab him. He'll be in jail sooner and we won't have to wait on the warrant."

Cissy sat on the couch. "I never thought about it, but it could speed things up."

"I'm going to sleep better now after what Juanita said about him waiting for us to leave." Missy picked up a thank you card and opened it to start writing in it. "Yes, I'm going to rely on God's protection and not let the evil one put fears in me."

"I agree." Cissy opened her book.

Chapter 17

The next morning, they left the house as usual. Cissy was dropped off at the daycare and then Missy and Juanita went to school.

Less than a half hour after the sisters left the house, Delgado's SUV went slowly past the house. Stephanie sat at the monitors watching and called the chief. "Delgado's back, Chief."

"There are two unmarked cars in the area keeping tabs on him. I don't think Delgado will park near the house, so he'll have to walk back. Keep watching the monitors. We have it under control."

"Okay, Chief." Stephanie hung up and smiled at Teresa. "I think Delgado is going to jail today."

Teresa stood by the desk looking over Stephanie's shoulders at the monitors. "Yep, I see him approaching by way of the backyard. I guess he didn't want neighbors to see him."

"He's being very bold, I'd say. I'll call the chief again," Stephanie said.

"Delgado's in the backyard, Chief."

"I know. I'm in contact with the team leader.

Call you back when we've got him. Stay upstairs by the monitors and you'll see it all go down." The chief hung up.

Teresa pointed to the image of the backyard where the policemen were coming up behind the fence as Delgado neared the back door. "You've done it now, Delgado. Just open the door and we've got you."

On the monitor, the two policewomen could see the back door. They heard the window glass break in the door and the crunch of Delgado's footsteps on the broken pieces. They held their breath as they watched the police creep up to the back door and then they heard, "Police! Put up your hands and don't move."

Stephanie and Teresa moved toward the bedroom door at the same time. By the time they arrived downstairs, Delgado was in handcuffs, and a policeman was reading the Miranda to him.

"Nice job, Ernie," Stephanie told the policeman holding Delgado's arm.

"We'll take him downtown and book him for unlawful entry." The policeman grabbed the suspect's arm. "Move."

"Great. Glad y'all were in the area." Teresa stepped back so the policeman and Delgado could leave the house.

Stephanie locked the front door behind them while Teresa went to the back door to assess the damage.

"As soon as the investigators are finished with the crime scene, we'll have to call someone to fix the broken glass." Teresa let out a sigh. "I'm glad that's over."

They both went back upstairs to make the call to Juanita.

* * *

Juanita ended the phone call and nodded to Missy.

Missy moved away from the student she had been helping and asked, "What happened?"

"He's on his way to the station after being caught inside your house."

"Did he get anything?"

"No, he didn't have a chance. They had him a minute after he entered, and he was very surprised." Juanita smiled at Missy. "You'll be able to sleep good tonight."

Missy smiled. "Yes, I will."

* * *

As soon as Cissy exited the daycare, Missy jumped out of the car and embraced her in a hug.

"He's in jail!" Missy cried out.

"Yay!" Cissy jumped up and down then took her twin's arm. "I want to hear all about it."

"I do too." Missy opened the car door. "Stephanie and Teresa will tell us what happened once we get home. I'm so relieved."

"It's a good day when a bad guy is taken off the street." Juanita smiled.

"Let's pick up pizza and salad on the way home to celebrate," Cissy suggested.

Missy nodded. "Sounds good to me."

* * *

A short time later, the three ladies entered the house carrying pizza, salad, and drinks.

"We're here," Juanita called out.

"We'll be down in a moment," Stephanie replied.

"I'll get plates, silverware, and salad dressing," Cissy said as she went into the kitchen.

Missy and Juanita placed the food and drinks on the dining room table.

A few minutes later, Teresa and Stephanie entered the dining room with smiles on their faces.

"Seeing Delgado in handcuffs was a relief to a tense day." Stephanie sat at the table looking at the pizza. "This pizza smells so good. I'm hungry."

"Y'all have to tell us everything," Cissy said as she came into the dining room.

"Let's pray first then we can listen to the details and eat at the same time." Missy sat at the table.

They joined hands and Missy prayed, "Dear Lord, thank you, thank you, thank you. I can't say it enough. Jesus has taken this day and made it a blessing to us. Now bless this food to the nourishment of our bodies.

In Jesus Christ's name I pray. Amen."

Missy looked at Stephanie and Teresa. "I've been imagining how it might have occurred since I heard about it this morning. Now, tell us the details, please."

"It happened so fast." Teresa took the plates from Cissy and passed them to the others around the table. "The chief had his team watching Delgado, and as soon as he broke the window in the back door and entered, they were right behind him."

"We heard the commotion after they entered the house and ran downstairs in time to see him being handcuffed." Stephanie grinned. "It ended quickly. Delgado was surprised."

"He broke the back window? I'll have to get it fixed." Missy took a slice of pizza and put it on her plate.

"It's already fixed. The chief had it repaired after the investigators left." Stephanie took a bite of pizza.

"I'll have to call the chief and thank him." Missy looked at Juanita. "I'm glad he's in jail. How long do you think he'll be there?"

"Not sure." Juanita spooned salad onto her plate. "It'll depend on how high the judge sets the bail. It may be just overnight."

"What? Oh no." Missy stopped abruptly with her fork midair. "I was hoping he wouldn't get bail. Do you think the marshal will have any say on how high the bail will be set?"

"At this point, Delgado will only be charged

with breaking and entering." Juanita served herself a slice of pizza. "If the warrant for the money-laundering charge is issued while he's in jail, the bail could be higher."

"At least, you can have a good night's sleep knowing Delgado's behind bars," Stephanie commented to Missy.

"Yep. We both can sleep better tonight." Cissy smiled at her sister.

"The chief will update me when Delgado goes before the judge which will probably be in the morning." Juanita looked around the table. "We'll continue with the surveillance until we're told it's not necessary."

"I appreciate everything y'all are doing for us." Missy smiled at the policewomen. "You've made me feel safe."

Cissy held up her glass in a toast. "To all of you ladies for the protection you've given us."

"Amen." Missy raised her glass. "You've helped keep me from freaking out at every noise I heard."

"It's our job." Juanita lifted her glass to Missy's. "But it's been a pleasure getting to know you both. Now, can we drop all of this and finish eating?"

Missy gave a little laugh. "Yes, of course."

Everyone ate their dinner and then the conversation turned to Missy's wedding plans.

Missy smiled. "I have a wonderful future mother-in-law who is taking care of the details as planned by my mother and myself. She knows what's going on and calls daily to check on me."

Cissy looked at Stephanie and Teresa. "You should see Missy's wedding dress. It's beautiful."

"Tell us about it, Missy." Stephanie took a drink of her soda.

Missy smiled as the image of her dress entered her mind. "It's a simple cut with tiny roses embroidered on the bodice. There are pearl buttons up the back which I'll need help fastening." Missy smiled at her sister. "The veil also has tiny roses in it."

Cissy continued, "The bridesmaid's dresses are a rose color with three-quarter sleeves and roses to match Missy's dress."

Missy nodded. "All the dresses are beautiful, just like the ladies who will be in them." She looked at her twin. "My best friend, Becky, and all my sisters will be in the wedding."

"Wow, it's going to be a big wedding party," Teresa exclaimed. "How many people have you invited?"

"It started out small but became larger as our mothers prepared the invitation list." Missy chuckled. "We've sent out a hundred and fifty invitations, but I don't know how many RSVPs we have so far."

Cissy started picking up the pizza boxes. "The day will be so exciting. Our sister, Gayle, is getting married in a few weeks, but it's a lot smaller."

"Oh my," Missy gasped. "I'd forgotten about her wedding coming so soon." She looked at Juanita. "You may be attending with me if Delgado gets out of jail."

Juanita nodded. "Let's just see what happens tomorrow, and then we'll make plans regarding your sister's wedding."

"I'm praying Delgado stays in jail," Missy said.

"We are, too," Stephanie chimed in.

Chapter 18

The morning after Delgado's arrest, Missy awoke refreshed. It was the best night's sleep she'd had since before the first break-in. She showered, dressed, and was combing her hair when her cell phone rang.

"Hello," Missy answered.

Ryan replied. "Hello, Beautiful, how are you doing?"

Missy shrieked with joy. "I'm great now. I've longed to hear your voice."

"Sorry, I couldn't call since I returned to base. We immediately went out on patrol. How are you doing, really?"

"I'm okay." Missy stammered wondering if she should tell him what had been happening.

"You don't sound sure," Ryan said after he heard the worry in her voice.

"Really, I am. You surprised me." Missy tried to keep her feelings intact. "I'm still trying to get used to my parents not being here. It's a blessing, though having Cissy with me."

"You know you can call Mom anytime you need

to."

"Yes, I know. Your mother has been a big help with the wedding and she calls every day to check on me." Missy sat on her bed. "She organized the shower and it was wonderful. We've so many great friends and the gifts they gave us filled the living room."

"Wow, I'm looking forward to seeing everything, but mostly I'm looking forward to holding you in my arms again."

"Me, too," Missy smiled at the thought. "How are things going with you?"

"You know I can't tell you much, but the patrol didn't have any problems while we were out. Missy, I love . . ." *static* . . . "so much . . ." *static.* "Can you . . ."

"Ryan, I didn't hear all you said." Missy's voice cracked with emotions.

"Connection bad, sorry . . . call . . . soon . . . bye." The phone went dead.

Missy slowly laid her phone on the dresser. She frowned, but her smile returned as she remembered Ryan's voice.

"Dear Lord, please keep Ryan safe and bring him home to me soon," Missy prayed. She picked up her brush and finished combing her hair. She smiled at her reflection. *I need to remember, Jesus Christ is with me and I can be strong through everything if I keep my eyes on Him.* She went downstairs and when she entered the kitchen, she found Cissy busy pouring water into the coffee pot.

"Good morning." Cissy looked at her sister.

"What are you smiling about?"

"Ryan." Missy placed her hand on her heart. "He just called me."

"I'm so happy for you. He's okay, right?"

"Yes, he's been on patrol and couldn't call before now. We didn't get to talk long. Lost the connection, but hearing his voice made my day." Missy went to the cabinet and removed a cup. "I'm going to have some tea. Want some or are you having coffee?" She pointed to the coffee maker.

"The coffee is for our friends upstairs. The kettle is already heating." Cissy took the tea bags out of the cabinet and handed them to Missy. "Juanita is making her daily backyard inspection."

Missy picked out a chai tea bag and put it in her cup. "Really? I didn't think she would need to do that anymore with Delgado in jail."

Cissy shook her head, "I guess she still needs to make sure everything's okay." She took the kettle off the burner, poured the hot water into her twin's cup and then into her own. "Do you think we'll hear anything today about Delgado getting bail or not?"

"I can answer your question." Juanita entered the kitchen from the backyard. "He should go before the judge this morning, and the chief said he'll let me know what happens."

"Do you think he'll get bail?" Missy asked.

"Depends on the judge. The chief and DA are trying to get the warrant to the judge, so he can have all the information about what's going on and why

Delgado broke into your house." Juanita took a cup from the cabinet and poured coffee into it. "We'll wait and see. It's never fast like it is on TV shows."

Missy smiled at Juanita. "Ryan called me this morning."

"Did you tell him what's going on?" Juanita looked at Missy over the rim of her cup as she took a sip.

"No, we didn't have much time to talk, and I didn't want him to worry about me." Missy leaned against the counter and sighed. "He said this was the first chance he had to call, and the connection wasn't very good."

"I think you did the right thing." Juanita refilled her cup. "Ryan needs to concentrate on his duties and stay safe."

"I know. I pray for him every day." Missy set her cup on the counter. "I think he heard the worry in my voice, but I told him I was surprised by his call."

Cissy looked at her twin. "So, did you sleep better last night? I know I did."

"Yes, I did." Missy opened the refrigerator and looked inside. "I'm so hungry this morning. What should we have for breakfast?"

"I'll eat whatever you cook." Juanita grinned. "I haven't had such good food in a long time. You may not know, but I'm not handy in the kitchen."

"I did notice you *do* eat anything we make." Cissy went to the refrigerator and looked over Missy's shoulder. "I could make pancakes." She turned and looked at Juanita. "Sound good?"

Juanita nodded. "I love pancakes. I'll go upstairs and tell the others and inform them everything is all right outside."

"Okay, it'll take a few minutes." Cissy went to the stove and took out the flat skillet. She glanced at her sister. "Missy, could you get me the eggs and milk?"

Missy retrieved the items her sister requested and set them on the counter. "I'm praying for the judge to not grant bail."

"Me, too." Cissy took a bowl out of the cabinet, turned and looked at her twin. "Praying this is the day we can be rid of all the danger."

Missy opened the pantry. "I'll get the syrup and set the table. Are you going to put the pancakes on one plate or individual plates?"

"I'll put them on separate plates, so the ladies can eat while it's hot." Cissy mixed the batter. "I think they all enjoy the meals." She winked at her sister.

Missy nodded in agreement and placed the plates by the stove. "Mom taught me how to cook when I was a preteen. I wonder if the policewomen know how?"

Cissy shrugged as she poured batter onto the griddle. "My mom taught me when I was young also, and I love preparing food for others. It's just the cleanup I'm not thrilled about."

"I love it all. I spent a lot of time with Mom here in the kitchen. I think we had the best talks while cleaning up." Missy looked sad for a moment then it changed into a happy face. "I remember some of the discussions we had, or should I say debates? She had a point of view I didn't always see."

"My mom and I have had some of those moments." Cissy flipped the pancakes on the griddle and turned to Missy. "Go tell everyone breakfast is ready."

* * *

Throughout the day while teaching class, Missy kept glancing out the window at Juanita sitting in her car. She didn't see any indication Juanita received a phone call from the chief. Finally, the last bell rang, and Missy gathered her purse and headed toward the back of the classroom where Juanita stood waiting for her.

Juanita started shaking her head. "I haven't heard anything yet."

"But I thought you said Delgado would go before the judge this morning." Missy collapsed in a chair by door.

"I know, but I have no idea how many other cases were on the docket today. The chief and DA may be getting the case delayed until the warrant comes in."

"It's stressful not knowing what's going on." Missy groaned then stood. "I'm not very patient, am I?"

"When it comes to the legal system, you have to be patient as there's always a delay." Juanita followed

Missy out of the classroom door. "They have court until four, so maybe we'll still hear something soon."

"I hope so." Missy walked toward the exit when she heard Juanita's phone ring.

"Hello." Juanita answered, looked at Missy, and gestured with her head to go back into the classroom. "Yes, Chief."

Missy stood by watching as Juanita listened to what was being said to her.

Juanita grinned as her face brightened. "Thanks, for calling, Chief."

Missy gave Juanita a hopeful look. "What happened?"

"Delgado is staying in jail."

"Yay!" Missy jumped with joy. "Let's go get Cissy and tell her. This is such good news."

* * *

Juanita and Missy left the school and headed to Cissy's workplace when her name appeared on Missy's ringing phone.

"Have you heard anything?" Cissy asked when Missy answered the call.

"Yes, we're on our way and will tell you the good news in person." Missy smiled.

"What? You said good news, right?" Cissy asked.

"Yes, Delgado is staying in jail."

Cissy shrieked with delight. "I'm so happy. We need to celebrate."

Missy held her phone away from her ear and looked at Juanita. "Can you tell she's happy?" Missy spoke into the phone, "I agree, we need to do something. We'll be there in a few minutes and then decide what to do."

"Okay, got to go. See you in a few." Cissy ended the call.

Missy put her phone in her purse and rubbed her ear. "She shrieked so loud, my ear is still ringing."

"I heard her." Juanita glanced at Missy. "Are you okay?"

"Yes, I wasn't expecting her to shriek."

"You should have, because you did the same thing." Juanita chuckled. "I was just lucky it wasn't through the phone."

"I guess we're happy. So, will this be the end of you being with us?"

"It does look like it." Juanita stopped the car at a red light. "If the chief thinks we don't have to protect you any longer, we could leave tonight."

"Oh no, not tonight." Missy sighed. "Do you think y'all can go out with us before you pack up?"

"I'll see what the chief says when we get back to your house." Juanita turned at the next corner and pulled into the daycare parking lot where Cissy worked.

Cissy came running out the door and nearly bumped into a mom entering the daycare. "Sorry, so sorry."

The woman stepped back, and watched Cissy

continue running. "Hey, slow down before you hurt someone!"

As Cissy opened the car door, she shouted back to the woman, "Sorry." She sat in the backseat and grabbed Missy's shoulder. "I'm so happy."

Missy chuckled. "I'm happy, too, but you need to be careful. Poor woman."

"I told her I was sorry." Cissy buckled her seat belt. "Tell me everything."

"The chief only told me Delgado was denied bail and is staying in jail." Juanita pulled away from the curb. "He said he'll call back later to tell me what's next."

"We still need to celebrate." Cissy leaned forward. "Can we all go out to eat?"

"Let me see what the chief says first and go from there." Juanita glanced into the rearview mirror. "But I think we can probably go out to eat."

"Yay!" Missy and her twin said at the same time.

Juanita grinned and shook her head.

Chapter 19

"It seems strange not having Juanita with us, doesn't it?" Missy asked her sister as the two of them got into the car to go to work.

"Yes, I miss them not being around." Cissy buckled her seat belt. "Dinner was fun last night with everyone."

Missy started the car. "They're really nice. I'm glad we were able to spend some fun time with all of them together. We either had one or two with us at all times but all three together was fun."

"When do you think they'll come back to get their equipment?"

"Juanita said in a few days." Missy backed the car out of the driveway. "The chief is going to leave most of the cameras for me. Juanita's going to show me how to operate the system after it's connected to my computer."

"He's really nice," Cissy commented. "Was he good friends with your dad?"

"Yes. They go back a long way," Missy replied. "They were in high school together."

"It's comforting having him look out for you." Cissy flipped the sun visor down to look in the mirror. "I'm thinking about getting my hair cut short. What do you think?"

Missy chuckled. "I was thinking the same thing about my hair, but not real short."

Cissy smiled at her sister. "We can go together. I want it done before Gayle's wedding, so it won't look just cut. You know what I mean?"

"Yes, I do. It takes me a few days after a haircut before I can get it looking the way I want it to." Missy stopped in front of the daycare and put the car in park. "Where do you go to get your hair done?"

"I don't have anyone special, do you?" Cissy unbuckled her seatbelt.

"Yes, I do. I go to Monika. She's been my hair stylist for as long as I can remember. Momma went there, too." Missy blinked back a tear. "Do you want me to make an appointment for us?"

"Okay with me." Cissy opened the car door. "Now since we're free from being restricted to the house, we can go anytime. It'll be interesting to see if she can do our hair different from each other since our hair is so much alike."

"I'll call on my break and set it up." Missy smiled. "She doesn't know about you, so I'll have to explain. I'll tell her we're twins but don't want the same hairstyle."

"I'll see you later." Cissy gave a little wave as she exited the car. "You know my schedule."

"Okay." Missy watched her twin and sighed. *It does feel good being on my own. I feel a peace from God.* She started singing, "Today's the first day of the rest of my life, and I'm going to be glad in it and trust in God."

***

Missy parked her car at the school and was about to step out when her phone rang. "Hello."

"This is Rodney Sims."

"Oh, what can I do for you?" She closed the car door for privacy.

"I have some forms I need you to sign so all the property from the estate can be transferred to your name. Can you come by my office sometime this week?"

"Yes, I'm available on Thursday." Missy pulled paper and a pen from her purse.

"Great, I'll see you then."

"Ah, Mr. Sims, I need to ask you a question."

"Of course. I think I know what the question is concerning. Your adoption, right?"

"Yes." Missy shifted in her seat. "It's been quite a surprise. Richard told me you knew about it."

"I did know and encouraged your parents to tell you when you were younger, but your father kept putting it off."

"Do you know why?"

"Your father felt you would want to find your biological family."

"So, he knew about my sisters?"

"No, he didn't know you had any living relatives. Your father thought telling you would change how you loved them. You would want to know what happened to your biological parents and how you ended up being adopted."

"Isn't wanting to know only normal? My love for them wouldn't have changed. Daddy was the only father I remember. Some memories of my family have been coming back since I've been with my sisters, but nothing regarding my birth father."

"Your father doted on you and didn't want anything to change your relationship with him. I think it stemmed back to his childhood."

"I know he was an only child, but why would it change my feelings for him?"

"Did you know your father was adopted also?"

Missy gasped. "No!"

"Well, he was, and when he found out, he felt differently toward his parents and didn't want you to feel as he had felt."

"I think maybe I understand better." Missy looked at her watch. "Mr. Sims, can we talk some more on Thursday? I have to get to work now."

"Yes, of course. What time can you come?"

"How about one o'clock?" Missy made a note of the time.

"Great, I'll tell my assistant to expect you."

* * *

After class, Missy drove to pick up her sister. *I have so much to tell Cissy. There are so many questions regarding my father now.*

She sat waiting for Cissy to come out while mulling over what she had learned.

Cissy opened the car door, slid into the seat, and saw a frown on her twin's face. "Hey, what's wrong?"

Missy blinked. "What? Oh, nothing. I got a call from my parents' lawyer, Mr. Sims."

"What did he want?" Cissy fastened her seat belt.

"He has some papers for me to sign. I'm going to his office on Thursday." Missy pulled the car away from the curb. "I had a chance to ask a couple of questions regarding my adoption and why my parents never told me."

"What did he say?" Cissy asked and placed her bag on the floor board.

"He told me he'd encouraged them to tell me."

Cissy shrugged her shoulders. "Why the frown on your face?"

"Sorry, I'm still a little stunned at what I learned about my father." Missy stopped at the stop sign and turned right. "He told me my father was adopted."

"What? Wow, I didn't see that coming." Cissy lowered the sun visor. "You didn't know?"

"No." Missy glanced at her twin.

"Did Mr. Sims tell you anything else?"

"He said they didn't tell me because my father thought it would change how I felt for them."

"Being adopted didn't change how I felt toward my adoptive parents. I think it made me love them more." Cissy smiled. "They chose me, and I love being wanted."

"You do have great parents, and so did I." Missy sighed. "I don't think knowing about being adopted and the reason why would change my love for them."

Missy drove into her driveway. "I never knew his parents. They died before David was born. Daddy always spoke lovingly about them." She turned to Cissy. "What did you do when you found out?"

"I had some questions, like why I was put up for adoption, but the only answers they had were my parents had died. I did wonder a lot at first about my real parents—what they were like, where did we live, and what did they do for a living. But as time went on, I guess it was something I put in the back of my mind."

Missy opened the car door. "I'm going to write down questions to ask Mr. Sims when I see him on Thursday. Oh, by the way, our hair appointment is on Friday. Hope you didn't have any plans."

Cissy picked up her purse. "Friday sounds good. Hey, here's a novel idea—we can make plans to do something fun instead of staying around the house."

Missy smiled at Cissy over the top of the car. "To even think about doing something besides staying home and safe. I like the idea of freedom."

The sisters reached the front door. "Let's order a pizza tonight. I don't feel like cooking, do you?"

"Pizza sounds good and so does not cooking." Missy unlocked the door. "Order, and I'll pay. You know what I like, the same as you." She chuckled.

Chapter 20

Stephanie walked to the front door and rang the doorbell. She waited for an answer, then she called out, "Missy, its Stephanie. Are you home? I need to talk to you." Stephanie looked through the small side window by the door but couldn't see anyone. She listened but heard nothing. *Something's wrong.* She went back to her car and drove down the street, stopping a few houses away. She called the chief on her cell phone. "Sir, something's wrong at Missy's house."

"Why do you think so?"

"I went to talk to Missy. Her car is in the driveway, lights on in the house, but no one answered the door. I called out my name."

"Okay, where are you now?"

"I'm parked a little way down from her house." Stephanie looked over her shoulder to see if she could see Missy's house. "I can see the front door but there's not any movement."

"I'm on my way but call Juanita. She's closer than I am."

"I will, Chief." Stephanie ended the call and

speed dialed Juanita's number.

Juanita picked up after the first ring. "Hi, what's going on?"

"The chief said to call you because I think there's trouble at Missy's house."

"What kind of trouble?"

Stephanie looked out the back window again. "Not sure. It looks like they're home, but no one answered the door."

"I'm not far away. Be there in about five minutes."

Stephanie started praying, "Lord, if you can hear me. Place your angels around them and keep them safe."

* * *

The twins sat in chairs in the dining room. Their hands bound behind them. "What do you want from us?" Missy asked with a tremor in her voice.

"Well, little lady, one of you has something my boss wants, and I'm here to get it." The man standing before them wore a ski mask with only his eyes and mouth visible. His dark eyes looked evil; his muscular frame sported a dragon tattoo on his left arm.

"I don't know what you're talking about." Missy looked him in the eye. "Tell me what it is and if I have it, I'll give it to you."

"Well, aren't you nice?" The man walked around the table getting closer to Missy. "Is there anyone else besides your friend Stephanie who might come to the door tonight?"

"No, we weren't expecting anyone except a pizza delivery." Missy looked at the pizza on the table then at Cissy. "Sometimes she just drops by to hang out with us."

"She's a good friend of ours," Cissy continued with a shudder in her voice. "She's over here all the time."

"For your sake and for hers, she'd better not come back." He pointed a knife at them and asked, "So, which one of you is Missy?"

"I . . . I am," Missy stammered with a quiver in her voice.

"Okay, now tell me, where's your laptop?"

Missy looked puzzled. "Why do you want it?"

He sneered, "If you really want to know, my boss thinks your daddy sent you a video with some information which would put my boss in hot water."

"I haven't seen any video from my father." A tear ran down Missy's cheek as she moved her shoulders to get them in a more comfortable position. "My father died a few weeks ago, so he wouldn't have sent an email."

"I want to take a look anyway." He bent over the table and stared Missy in the eye. "I'll ask you again. Where's your laptop?" He slammed his hand on the table.

The twins jumped in their chairs.

"It's . . . it's in my room on the desk." Missy shivered because of the closeness of the man and his foul breath.

"Now we're getting somewhere." He leaned back. "Where's your room?"

"Up . . . upstairs to the right, the . . . the last door." Missy squirmed in her seat trying to put distance between her and the man.

"You ladies stay right where you are, and I'll be back in a minute." He chuckled as he walked out of the room. "As if you can go anywhere."

When Cissy heard him going upstairs, she whispered to Missy, "Do you think Stephanie knows something's wrong?"

"It's what I've been praying since I heard her voice. I think God sent her here to help." Missy's eyes filled with tears again, and she shook her head. "I can't let him see me crying."

"You're doing a great job keeping calm. Better than me." Cissy shifted in her chair and smiled. "And I thought I was the courageous one."

Missy looked at her twin and back toward the hallway. "He's coming back."

Cissy nodded. "I'm praying hard."

The man entered the dining room carrying the laptop. "Now all I need is your password."

Missy looked at the man. "I don't think you'll find anything."

"That's for me to find out." He set the laptop on the table and pulled out a chair. "Give me the password, or this twin won't look so much like you anymore." He pulled out his knife and motioned to Cissy.

"Okay, okay, don't do anything to her," Missy pleaded. "It's 'Jesus saves.'"

"A Bible pusher, are you?" He started typing in the password. "I don't think your Jesus will be saving you tonight. Now let's see what I can find."

He opened the email and started scrolling down. "Well, well, well, look what I found, an email from your old man with an attachment." He clicked on the attachment. "Let's see what he sent you."

A picture of a building with beautiful gardens appeared on the screen. "What's this?" He asked as he turned the screen, so Missy could see it.

Missy looked and nodded at the screen. "It's a picture of the gardens where my father wants me to have my wedding reception." She shook her head. "I told you, he didn't send me anything."

The man turned the laptop back toward him and continued looking at the emails.

A slight click came from the direction of the front door and Missy moved in her chair to try to camouflage the sound. The man sat engrossed in looking at the screen and didn't hear the noise.

"I don't see any other emails with attachments. He must've put it on your computer in another file." He shut down the laptop. "I'm taking this, so I can look at it when I have more time."

"No, you can't take my computer," Missy proclaimed as she looked over his shoulder and saw Stephanie with a finger to her lips. "All my school work is on it. How can I turn in the paper due tomorrow if you have it? I haven't printed the pages."

"Isn't that a shame? You're going to get an F for not turning in the paper." He sheathed his knife and with a grin on his face, picked up the laptop.

"Police!" Stephanie shouted as she stepped into the dining room, gun pointed at the intruder. "Slowly put the laptop on the table and put your hands in the air. You're under arrest."

The man's grin faded. He slowly did as he was told but as he started raising his hands in the air, quickly turned, and moved toward Stephanie. He attempted to grab her gun but stopped after seeing Juanita in the hallway, pointing her firearm directly at his chest.

"As she said, hands in the air; down on your knees." Juanita nodded to Stephanie. "Cuff him."

Stephanie holstered her weapon, pulled his hands behind him, and put the handcuffs on his wrists. "Let's see who we have here." She jerked off the man's mask.

"Joey." Juanita chuckled. "Well, isn't this something? We had a feeling your boss was involved but I couldn't connect the dots until now. Thanks for helping."

Stephanie moved behind Missy and Cissy and cut the ties binding their hands. "Are y'all okay?"

Tears ran down Missy's cheeks. She rubbed her wrists and nodded. "Yes, thank the Lord and you, too."

"I really didn't know how we were going to get out of this one." Cissy embraced her sister. "It sure was good hearing you at the door, Stephanie."

They both jumped when the front door banged open. The chief entered the dining room with his weapon drawn. "Looks like y'all got it under control." He looked at Joey and smiled. "We got you now, Joey. Let's see you get out of this one."

Joey looked at the chief. "I'll be out before you know it."

"Ah, but we do have the goods on you and your boss." The chief looked at Missy. "A little video on a thumb drive says it all."

Missy sighed. "I didn't tell him about the thumb drive."

"It'll put them both in jail for a long time." The chief turned to Juanita. "Now, get him out of here and read him his rights. Don't want anything to go wrong with this arrest."

Juanita said the Miranda as she led Joey down the hallway where two policemen waited to take him to the police station.

The chief walked over to Missy. "Are you okay?"

"Yes, just very scared and grateful for the rescue."

"I'll need to get a statement from you and your sister. We can do it now or you can come to the station in the morning."

"I'd like to get it over now, Chief." Missy looked at Cissy. "Okay with you?"

"Yes, while it's fresh in my mind but I don't think I'll forget this anytime soon," Cissy agreed. "I don't want to leave out anything."

"Shall we go into the family room?" The chief motioned for them to go ahead of him. "Stephanie, get Juanita so she can record the information."

Stephanie returned to the family room with Juanita. "I'll also give my statement."

The chief nodded. "Let's get theirs first, and afterwards you can give yours. Missy, you start. Tell me how he got in the house?"

Missy looked at Juanita and inhaled deeply. "We ordered pizza to be delivered."

"And you didn't look to see who was at the door, right?" Juanita jumped in.

"Yes." Missy looked embarrassed. "I opened the door expecting the pizza delivery man but was shocked to see a man wearing a ski mask. I couldn't move. He barged in with a knife in his hand and shut the door."

The chief turned to Cissy. "Where were you, Cissy?"

"When the doorbell rang, Missy went to answer it, and I walked into the kitchen to get plates." She looked at her hands, which were still shaking, and continued. "I heard the commotion and picked up the phone on the wall to dial 911 when he said, 'Where's your sister? Hope she's not trying to be heroic.' I put the phone down, wishing I hadn't left my cell phone in the family room, and stepped into the hallway, so he could see me."

Missy reached over and took Cissy's hand, then

looked back at the chief. "Sorry, Chief, we thought we were safe and didn't take precautions."

"What happened next?" Juanita asked as she recorded everything.

"He told me to move and gestured with the knife toward Cissy." Missy squeezed her twin's hand. "I was so scared. We both were."

"I tried to think of what I should do without getting either of us hurt." Cissy looked at her sister. "I couldn't see anything but the knife."

"The masked man looked in each room as we moved down the hallway toward the kitchen, but when he saw the dining room, he told us to sit in the chairs on the far side of the room." Missy wiped a tear off her cheek. "I was so scared I could barely walk."

"He handed me zip ties and told Missy to put her hands behind her back." Cissy reached up and touched her twin's cheek as a tear fell. "I did what I was told, but I had problems getting the ties into the slot and when I did, I didn't tighten it real tight."

"I was shaking so much she couldn't keep my hands still," Missy told everyone. "He ordered Cissy to sit, and he put zip ties on her wrists. I could see the pain on her face as he pulled it tight."

"He checked Missy's hands and tightened the ties then said, 'You didn't think I would check, did you?' He laughed when he said it." Cissy rubbed her red wrist where the ties had been.

Missy looked over to the chief. "Then the doorbell rang, and we heard 'Pizza delivery.' I really didn't know they announced themselves at the door."

"The intruder chuckled and said, 'Dinner's here.' Then he went into the hallway. I heard him as he opened the door. He was joking with the delivery guy." Missy rubbed her sweaty hands on her pants. "The man must've taken off the mask when he opened the door, but when he returned the mask covered his face again. He dropped the pizza box on the table, opened it, and took a slice and took a bite through the slit over his mouth."

"My stomach rumbled, and he said, 'Want a piece? Oh, forgot your hands are tied. Sorry, but I paid for it, so it's mine.'" Cissy pushed a strand of her blond hair behind her ear. "He was enjoying scaring us."

"After taking another slice of pizza, the masked man sat down and looked at each of us." Missy glanced toward the dining room. "Then he started asking questions about a video my dad was supposed to have emailed to me. I told him I didn't know of any video, but he insisted I wasn't telling the truth. I didn't tell him about the thumb drive the marshal took. He kept saying there's info, and he wanted it."

"He became agitated when the doorbell rang again." Cissy looked at Stephanie. "When I heard your voice, I knew you would help us. I prayed, you'd figure out something was wrong."

"With the car in the driveway and the lights on in the house, I knew it wasn't right." Stephanie looked at the chief. "I called you right after I moved my car down the block where I could still see the house."

The chief looked back at Missy. "What did Joey do next?"

"He wanted my laptop," Missy replied. "I told him where to find it. While he was gone, we tried to get out of the ties, but they were too tight. He came back, demanding I give him the password. I reluctantly gave it to him. Then he started looking through my emails."

"I heard the front door unlock with a soft click and moved in my chair to make noise to help cover up the sound." Cissy shifted on the couch to demonstrate. "Missy kept him talking about what he was looking for, so we could get details, all the while, praying Stephanie was coming down the hallway and would hear."

Stephanie looked at Juanita. "You arrived just as I was trying to figure out how to get in the house. As we entered, I heard the frustration in the perp's voice as he talked about trying to find the video."

Juanita looked at Missy. "I was on my way over here to return your door key." Taking the key out of her pocket, she placed it on the coffee table.

"Praise God you still had it." Missy smiled. "The crook was ready to leave with my laptop when Stephanie stepped into the dining room with her weapon pointed at him." She breathed a sigh of relief. "I was so happy to see you." She glanced at Juanita. "I didn't know you were here until he tried to escape. Thank you both so very much." A tear slipped down Missy's cheek and she gave a weary smile.

"I'm glad you two stayed calm and did what he

told you to do." The chief nodded to Stephanie and Juanita. "They're very good policewomen and I'm glad they came when they did. By the way, what were you doing here, Stephanie?"

Stephanie looked at the chief and then at Missy as she inhaled, "I wanted to talk to Missy about something."

"What?" the chief asked.

"I wanted to continue a conversation we had while I was here." Stephanie looked a little nervous.

Looking between Missy and Stephanie, the chief asked, "Conversation about what?"

"Well . . . err . . . it's personal, Chief," Stephanie replied.

"Personal? Maybe you can talk to her tomorrow." The chief looked at the two sisters. "I think these girls need to get some rest right now. Do you want Stephanie and Juanita to stay the night?"

"Yes, please, if it's possible." Missy put her hands together as in prayer. "I know I'll sleep better knowing they're here."

"All right, let's make this happen." The chief looked at Juanita and Stephanie. "Do you have any problems staying the night?"

"No, sir," Juanita answered, "I always keep a bag in my car, so I'll be ready for anything."

"I'm good." Stephanie smiled at Missy.

The chief stood. "I'm sure this is the last of the threats against you. We already have a warrant out for the arrest of Joey's boss, who's behind all of this.

Delgado was a pawn in this situation. The ring leader should be in jail tonight." He looked at Juanita and Stephanie. "Good job."

"Thanks, Chief." Stephanie smiled and looked at the twins. "I'm thankful it turned out as it did."

"Okay, these ladies are in your hands for the night." The chief indicated the twins. "I'll let you know when the arrest has been made on Joey's boss. Good night, ladies." He left the family room.

Missy and Cissy hugged each other again, then Missy turned to Stephanie and Juanita. "I can only praise God for hearing our prayers tonight. Words can't express how thankful I am for you both."

"I'm just glad I decided to come over here tonight." Stephanie looked at Missy. "I'd been thinking about our conversation." She glanced at Cissy and Juanita. "I've seen the way Missy handled this entire situation and how much she relies on God for everything. She told me about her faith in Him. I think I've seen it tonight as He used you and me to protect them."

Juanita nodded. "I've seen it also and told Missy I admire her strength and faith."

"God is good all the time...," Missy started.

"All the time, God is good." Cissy continued with a smile.

"I'd be very happy to continue our conversation with you, Stephanie. I know Jesus is working in your heart." Missy reached for Stephanie's hands. "You only have to ask."

Stephanie nodded.

Missy led Stephanie in the prayer of salvation and all four of the ladies said, "Amen" together. Tears of joy flowed down everyone's face.

Even Juanita was touched to be a part of the special moment.

Missy looked at Stephanie. "I must tell you, it won't be easy following Jesus in your daily life, but I'm always here if you need someone to talk to. You'll have trials, and how you respond will help grow your faith as you choose to trust in God."

Stephanie smiled at Missy. "If I can have only a tiny bit of the strength and faith you've shown these past weeks, I'm sure I'll be able to survive."

Juanita put her hand on Stephanie's shoulder. "You'll get some flak from some others on the police force because of this decision. I know. I've had to endure a lot because of my faith. I'm Catholic and my worship differs from Missy's, but in the end, we both believe in Jesus Christ." She smiled at Missy.

"If you get into a church and a small group for Bible Study, it'll help you to get grounded in the word of God." Missy gently touched Stephanie's arm. "Your work hours will hinder you some, but there's studies you can do on your own." Missy turned and picked up a book she had on the end table. "Here, I bought this before all this happened and haven't had a chance to start it. We can do it together if you like, when you have the time." She turned to her sister and asked, "Do you want to do it with us?"

"Yes, I just finished my last study and was looking for a new one." Cissy replied. "What's the name of the study?"

"*His Warrior Sisters, Owning Christ's Identity* by Linda Goldfarb. She's a friend of mine. The title seems to fit us, doesn't it? I'll get the books from Linda." Missy looked at Juanita. "Do you want to join us?"

"I'd be happy to join." Juanita smiled. "I haven't been in a small group study in a long time, mainly because of work." She spoke to Stephanie, "It'll take some coordination to get us here at the same time."

"God will work it out. He does miracles you know." Missy smiled while looking at each of the ladies. "I'm so happy He brought you both into my life. Not so happy about the circumstances, but if it hadn't happened, we'd never have met."

Everyone nodded realizing the truth in what Missy said.

Juanita cleared her throat. "I'll go get my bag from my car." She looked at Stephanie and asked, "Do you need to go home to get some things?"

"No, I'm like you. I have a bag in the car," Stephanie replied. "Let's get our things. Should we order another pizza?"

They all chuckled and nodded.

Chapter 21

A couple of days later, the doorbell rang. Missy approached the door and looked out the side window to see Chief Stone standing outside. She opened the door, and asked, "What brings you here, Chief?"

"May I come in?"

Missy stepped back and gestured for the chief to enter. "Yes, of course."

The chief walked in. "There's been some developments regarding the whole situation, and I wanted to tell you in person."

"Oh, okay. Let's go to the family room." Missy closed the door and walked down the hallway. "Cissy's here."

The chief followed Missy into the family room and nodded at Cissy. "Glad you're here. Since you've been a part of all of this, you should know what's happening."

"Please, sit here." Missy indicated the recliner. "I hope its good news you have for us." Missy sat on the couch beside her twin.

"It is good news." The chief cleared his throat as

he sat down. "Joey and Delgado turned state's evidence against their boss, who we've got in custody."

"Can you tell us who it is and what this was all about?" Cissy asked.

"I can only tell you so much because it is an open case." The chief looked at Cissy and then at Missy. "Delgado was laundering money at your father's bank for a man named Cartwright."

Missy gasped, "As in Cartwright's Lawncare Service?"

"The one and the same." The chief nodded.

"We use his service," Missy exclaimed.

"I know." The chief shifted in the chair. "It's his legit business. We've been monitoring his clients, so we can find out which ones were actual clients or a cover for dealing drugs."

"So, what my father had on the thumb drive implicated Cartwright?" Missy asked.

"Yes." The chief clasped his hands together.

"Can you tell us more about the evidence my father obtained?" Missy inquired.

"No, sorry." The chief sat back in the chair. "But I can tell you Delgado did sell houses. He had a knack at flipping houses and making a good profit."

"You mean Delgado was a realtor?" Missy asked with disbelief.

"Yes, and a good one too." The chief shook his head. "We're still trying to figure out what caused him to launder money for Cartwright."

"How did my father get Delgado to say anything

about Cartwright?" Missy asked.

"Your father didn't, directly. You see, when the marshal approached your father with a scheme to get information on Delgado's activities, he had microphones installed at the tellers' windows. When Delgado came in to make a deposit or withdrawal, your father was able to record what he said to the teller."

"Did the tellers know what was going on?" Missy leaned forward.

"No," the chief replied. "The tellers didn't even know there was a microphone at their station. Your father controlled it only when Delgado came into the bank."

Missy inhaled deeply. "I'm glad the tellers weren't involved. But isn't it illegal to record someone without them knowing it?"

"Yes, it is, but there's a sign posted in the bank stating transactions may be monitored and recorded." The chief shrugged. "So, the recording is legal."

"How does money laundering work?" Cissy asked.

"Delgado would come in with cash, usually around nine thousand dollars at a time. He'd tell the teller one of his clients paid him in cash and wanted to get it deposited as soon as he could because he didn't like walking around with so much money."

"Was this a cover?" Cissy asked.

"Yes and no." The chief looked at Cissy. "Cartwright would give Delgado cash to deposit which was from the drug money. Then a few days after each deposit, Delgado would come back into the bank, and get a bank check for seven to eight thousand dollars saying he needed it to cover cost of landscaping at the house he was flipping. Delgado used Cartwright's lawn service. But he'd pay Cartwright with the bank check which was from the drug money. Then Cartwright would deposit the check into his off-shore account. Money laundering."

"I had no idea how it all worked." Missy shook her head. "I don't understand why Cartwright just didn't deposit the cash."

"Cartwright couldn't send cash to an offshore account. He needed a check or wire transfer." The chief wiped his hand down his face. "It's confusing, and you don't have to worry about it."

"What happens now?" Missy asked. "Will we have to testify against Joey?"

"Joey took a deal, so there won't be a trial. So, no, you won't be testifying." The chief stood. "I know you probably have more questions, but remember, the man who was behind all this is behind bars and will be for a long time. The danger to y'all is over."

Missy and Cissy both sighed together.

The twins both stood. "Thanks, Chief for coming over and telling us," Missy said. "We've been wondering what was going on."

The chief smiled. "I wanted you to know so you can feel safe again."

"I appreciate it." Missy smiled slightly. "I have a question."

"I'll answer if I can."

"What did the investigation into the accident reveal?"

"I can answer that question." The chief looked down at the cap in his hands and then back to Missy. "It was determined the accident was just that, an accident. The man driving hit a patch of black ice and couldn't stop because he was speeding. He's been arrested and charged with vehicular manslaughter on three accounts."

"Oh, poor man." Missy gasped. "Will he be sent to prison?"

"He could, but it depends on the judge. This accident not only changed your life but his also." The chief touched Missy's shoulder. "He has already shown regret in his actions and pleaded guilty."

"Will I need to be at the trial?"

"Only if you want to face him and tell the judge how this has impacted you as a victim."

"A victim? I wasn't in the accident." Missy proclaimed.

"No, but because of his actions, your life has changed." The chief tapped his cap against his leg. "Missy, it's up to you. The DA will be calling you about the trial when it's scheduled. I must go now. You have my number and if anything, and I do mean *anything*, bothers you, call me."

"I will." Missy smiled.

"Well, it's nice seeing y'all again." The chief looked at Cissy. "Take good care of her until Ryan comes home."

Cissy nodded and glanced over at her sister. "We've been taking care of each other."

"Goodbye, ladies," The chief said as he turned and walked down the hallway.

Missy followed him to the door. "Is it okay if I keep in touch with Juanita and Stephanie?"

The chief opened the door and turned toward Missy. "Yes, it's okay. I know they're quite fond of you and Cissy."

"Thanks." Missy closed the door after the chief walked out.

"Thank you, Jesus, for this good news, and I lift up the man who caused the accident. Give him peace and help me to forgive him." Missy said out loud.

Chapter 22

Cissy knocked on the bedroom door. "Are you ready?"

"Yes, I'm coming." Missy opened the door. "Do I look okay?"

"Yes, you look lovely." Cissy twirled to show her dress. "How about me?"

"You look wonderful." Missy picked up her handbag. "I can't believe today is Gayle's wedding. So much has happened since I first heard the plans for it."

"I know. It seems like it was yesterday she told me about her engagement."

"I'm glad her fiancé returned home safe." Missy followed her twin downstairs. Her eyes teared up and she sniffled. "Sorry, I haven't heard from Ryan for a while. I'm worried."

Cissy stopped on the bottom step, turned, and looked at her sister. "Ryan's okay. He'll call when he can. Didn't you tell me, he can only call when he's back at base camp?"

Missy wiped her eyes with a tissue from her

purse. "Yes, I did. I need to remember to trust Jesus for Ryan's safety."

"I can't imagine what you're going through, but I'm here to listen when doubts come to mind." Cissy took the tissue from Missy's hand. "Let me touch up your makeup. I'm sure Ryan will call you soon."

Missy nodded and gave a small smile. "Enough of this, let's get to the wedding."

* * *

Sitting on the front pew with the other family members, Missy became aware of the uneasiness she felt. She sighed, *Dear Lord, I plead with you to keep Ryan safe and bring him home to me. I'm so afraid for his safety. Take this fear from me and give me a peace to know you are in control.*

The pianist started playing Canon in D which brought Missy's thoughts back to the event about to happen. She turned, and watched as her sisters, Dottie, Joy, and Cissy walked down the aisle to take their places alongside the pastor. The wedding march began, everyone stood, and turned toward the back of the church.

"Oh, she's beautiful," Missy whispered when she saw Gayle come into the view.

On the arm of her brother-in-law, Travis Walker, she walked to the altar where her future husband stood, beaming with a smile so big, it was contagious.

When it came time for Missy to do her part of

the ceremony, she stood at the same time as the mother of the groom and walked to the table at the side of the couple. They took a candle, nodded at each other, and touched their flames to light the ornate unity candle in the center of the table. Blowing out their candles, they replaced them in the holders, turned, smiled at the happy couple, then walked back to their seats.

My family is becoming larger. A month ago, my mom, dad, and brother were taken away from me, but God sent me sisters who would ease the loneliness in my heart. Thank you, Jesus, for your unfailing love.

Too soon the ceremony was over, and the newlyweds made their way back down the aisle, followed by the rest of the wedding party. Missy caught up with her sisters. "Wasn't it beautiful?"

"Yes, and yours will be too." Cissy hugged her twin.

Tears puddled in Missy's eyes. "I can only hope it will. Gayle is so radiant, and I can tell she deeply loves Tyler."

"They do love each other very much." Dottie turned and look toward the happy couple. "We need to get over to the receiving line, so the reception can begin."

The sisters walked toward the new couple, and Cissy looked back and saw Missy standing where they left her. She went back and said, "Come on, you're needed in the receiving line. You're part of this family, remember?"

Missy beamed. "It feels strange to be included.

Thanks for reminding me. I need to get used to having a family around, now." She hugged her sister and they followed the others to take their places beside the newlyweds.

Chapter 23

The next few weeks were busy as Missy and her future mother-in-law worked together to finalize the wedding plans. Cissy joined them as they went to the cake tasting.

"Which flavor of cake do you like best, Missy?" Mrs. Franklin asked as she took a bite of a classic white cake with a hint of raspberry flavoring.

"I do like the one you're tasting now, but I know Ryan likes chocolate." Missy gestured to the cake she was talking about. "Do you think we could have both?"

"Yes, you can. The white cake could be the main one and the chocolate, the groom's cake." Mrs. Franklin took a bite of the chocolate cake. "Yum, this is good."

"I know, I think it has a hint of cherry in it." Cissy took another bite and smiled at her twin. "Does Ryan like cherry, too?"

"I hadn't noticed the cherry flavor, but I think he'd like it." Missy turned to Mrs. Franklin. "What do you think, Katie?"

"I know Ryan loves cherry and chocolate

together because his favorite candy at Christmas time is chocolate covered cherries." Mrs. Franklin chuckled. "When he was little, I caught him with a whole box of the candy. I was able to keep him from making himself sick."

Missy smiled. "I think we have our cakes picked out. I would like to have the white cake decorated with white roses, of course, not real flowers but made from icing." She reached over to pick up the cake book on the table. "I saw one I liked in this book."

"I thought you wanted the same colors on the cake as in your wedding." Mrs. Franklin looked at the book to see what Missy was talking about. "Did you change your mind?"

"Yes." Missy turned a page in the book. "My mother loved white roses and I want to incorporate them into my wedding as a remembrance of her."

"You are such a good daughter." Mrs. Franklin patted Missy on her hand. "I'm so glad you'll soon become my daughter-in-law."

Missy blinked a tear from her eye. "Thank you, Katie."

"Is this the cake, Missy?" Cissy pointed to a picture of a three-layer cake, decorated in white icing with clusters of white roses trailing from the top down to the bottom layer.

"Yes, just what I want. I think it's elegant, don't you?" Missy looked between her sister and future mother-in-law.

"I think it's the perfect cake for your wedding."

Mrs. Franklin smiled and wrote down the name of the cake to give the shop owner.

"Missy, since you've changed the way the cake is decorated, do you want to change what flowers are in the wedding?" Mrs. Franklin asked.

"The bridesmaids will have the flowers I've already picked out, but I want my bouquet to be white roses with baby's breath." Missy stood. "We're off to the florist next, so I can tell her."

"This is so exciting." Cissy closed the cake book, took one last bite of her favorite red velvet cake, and stood. "Sis, thank you for letting me tag along while you finish the details of your wedding."

"I need all the help I can get making decisions, and I love having you with me." She hugged her twin. "Besides, you're the stand-in for Becky."

"I'm sorry your friend isn't here." Mrs. Franklin picked up her purse. "I tried to get this scheduled for when she was home, but with her finals she couldn't make it."

"I know." Missy sighed. "Becky wanted to be here so much, but her school schedule keeps her busy. She wants to get everything done so she can graduate and then concentrate on the wedding."

"She's always been such a good friend to you." Mrs. Franklin pointed to the counter. "There's the lady who was helping us. Let me show her what you want."

The two sisters lingered at the table, while Mrs. Franklin gave the cake details to the decorator.

"So, we'll go to the florist next and then the caterer." Cissy bounced with excitement. "I didn't get to help with this part of Gayle's wedding. This is fun."

Mrs. Franklin approached the sisters. "Are you ready to go to the florist?"

"We are," the twins answered.

Cissy chuckled, "Can you tell, I'm excited?"

* * *

After going to the florist and caterer, Mrs. Franklin drove the sisters back to Missy's home.

"Do you want to come in, Katie?" Missy asked as she opened the car door.

"Sorry, I must get home. David and I are going to a party this afternoon."

"Okay." Missy stepped out of the car, leaned down, and looked at her future mother-in-law. "Have a good time. Thank you for getting the details of the wedding finalized."

"You're more than welcome, dear. I'll be talking to you later this week."

The twins walked up to the house, turned, and watched her drive away.

"She's a nice lady. You're lucky to have such a caring future mother-in-law."

Missy unlocked the front door. "Yes, she's wonderful. I've always had a good relationship with Ryan's parents."

Cissy kicked off her shoes and picked them up.

"I'm going upstairs to get my house slippers, they're more comfortable."

"I'll be in the family room." Missy continued down the hallway. She stopped in the kitchen and called out to her twin, "Do you want something cold to drink?"

"Yes. I'd love a big glass of ice water."

"Okay." Missy took two glasses from the cabinet and started filling them with ice when her cell phone rang. She grabbed it from her purse and shrieked as she pushed the talk button. "Ryan!"

"Hello, Beautiful. How are you doing, my love?"

"Oh, Ryan." She ambled to the couch in the family room. "I'm so happy to hear from you. I was beginning to think something happened to you."

"Sorry about not calling," Ryan said. "We were out on patrol and ran into some trouble. It took us longer to get back to camp because a couple of my buddies were injured."

Missy gasped. "Are you hurt?"

"No, Sweetheart, I'm fine. Tired, but healthy," Ryan assured her.

"I pray for your safety every day."

"I could feel God's protection on me while we were out. My buddy next to me was shot in the leg."

"Oh." Missy gulped. "I'm sorry this happened to him or to any of the servicemen over there." She looked up and saw her twin standing in the door and mouthed, "Ryan."

Cissy nodded and went to the kitchen to finish

getting the drinks.

"Missy, I've wanted to hear your voice so much. I called as soon as I could."

"I've missed you, too." Missy put her hand over her heart. "I'm counting the days until you come home, sixty-three days until our wedding. I was with your mother today making final decisions on the cake, flowers, and caterer."

"I'm glad you're keeping busy. How's your student teaching going?" The connection crackled, "Missy, I'm losing you . . ." the static worsened. "I love you."

"I love you, too. So, happy to hear your voice." The call disconnected. Missy sat with the phone still to her ear listening, hoping to hear Ryan's voice again.

Her sister walked into the room with glasses of ice water and set them on the coffee table. "Lost connection?"

Missy nodded as she laid her phone in her lap. "He's okay. Thank you, Jesus." She looked at her sister. "He told me the guy next to him was shot in the leg. It could have been Ryan." Tears streaked down her face.

Cissy sat next to Missy and embraced her. "Don't think about the 'could haves,' just think about Ryan being surrounded by God's angels."

Missy reached for a tissue and wiped her face. "I know, I need to thank Jesus, and I do. My heart hurts not knowing what's going on over there, wherever he is. I can only pray for his safety. I'll also pray for the other men who were injured."

"Let's pray right now." Cissy took her arm from behind Missy's shoulders and clasped her twin's hands. "Dear Lord, Our Father of Protection. We're asking for You to keep watch over Ryan. Keep him safe and bring him home to Missy. We also ask for healing for the ones injured. You are in control. Please bring our focus back to You when we start to think of the 'what ifs.' Bless Ryan and his platoon and keep them out of harm's way. I lift Missy up to You. Give her a peace when she thinks of Ryan and reassure her, the You are going to bring Ryan home to her. In Jesus Christ's most precious name. Amen."

Missy hugged her sister. "Thank you for praying." She wiped her eyes. "God brought you back into my life when I needed you most. I don't think I could have gotten through these past weeks without you here. Words cannot express how thankful I am for you."

"What are sisters for? You have blessed me so much, seeing the strength of God work in you. I'm encouraged and thank Him daily for you."

They hugged each other again.

"Hearing Ryan's voice gave me such a relief." Missy grinned.

"I know you've been worried, but now you can relax knowing he's okay."

"I do feel the tension leaving me." Missy picked up her phone. "I need to call his mother and let her know I heard from him." Selecting her future mother-in-law's number on her cell, she took deep breaths until she answered. "Hi, Katie, I just heard from Ryan."

"Is he okay?" She could hear the relief in Mrs. Franklin's voice.

"Yes, he said their patrol ran into some trouble and a couple of the guys were shot, but he's fine."

"So glad you called to let me know you heard from him. Glad you caught me. We were just on our way out the door. Are you okay?"

"I'm feeling great now, since I've heard from him. Wished it was a longer conversation, but I'll take what I can get."

"Good. Sorry to be so abrupt but we really need to leave now, or we'll be late. I'll talk to you tomorrow. Bye."

"Bye." Missy ended the call.

"There's the smile I love to see," Cissy said.

Missy turned to her sister. "I haven't done much smiling lately, have I?"

"No, but I understand. Keep smiling, praying, and the days between now and your wedding will fly by."

"I hope so." Missy picked up her glass of water. "Thanks for finishing what I started."

"No problem." Cissy also took her glass from the coffee table. "You had other things more important."

The sisters clinked their glasses together, took a drink, and laughed.

Chapter 24

As the morning sun crept over her face, Missy awoke with a start, her heart pounding. Turning to look at the calendar on her desk, she swung her legs off the bed and remembered. *Today is my wedding day.* She smiled, jumped out of bed, and grabbed her robe on her way to the shower.

As Missy returned to her room from the bathroom, her twin came bounding up the stairs.

"I was wondering if you were going to sleep all day." Cissy chuckled. "There's nothing important going on today, is there?"

Missy grinned. "I'm so excited. I couldn't fall asleep last night for quite a while, but after I did, I had a wonderful dream."

"It must've been, your face is beaming, or is it just because of this special day?" Cissy asked.

"Maybe both." Missy rubbed the towel in her hand against her cheek. "In my dream, I was dressed in my wedding gown and my parents and David were hugging me. They were telling me to be happy in my new life. I think they were telling me to embrace the family God gave me after they went home to heaven. The dream brought me peace. It sure is different from the one I had the night before I learned about you and our other sisters."

"Isn't God wonderful?" Cissy declared. "He provides when we can't see the future."

"Yes, I don't know what I would've done if I didn't have God in my life. I wonder what other people rely on if they don't believe. I can't imagine going through what I have without Him."

"Well, God brought you to this day, and if we don't get going, you'll be late for your own wedding."

Missy giggled and did a happy dance. "I'm getting married today to the most wonderful man in the world. God blessed me so much and I feel overwhelmed." She twirled with a laugh. "Okay, let me get dressed and we'll get going."

* * *

The twins and Becky met the other sisters at the spa for a mani/pedi and their hair styled.

"This feels like *déjà vu,*" Cissy declared. "We came here on our first outing together."

"This time, we're getting ready for a wedding." Becky hugged Missy then stepped back. "So, bride-to-be, how are you going to have your golden blonde hair fixed?"

Missy touched the top of her head. "I think, I'll leave it down with curls on top."

"You told Mrs. Taylor, you were going to wear your hair down and she said the veil would fit nicely. Soft curls will make it look fancy," Becky agreed.

The spa manager, Lorraine, approached the group. "Is this the entire entourage for the wedding?"

"Yes," Becky answered as she took Missy by the shoulders and urged her to stand in front of everyone. "She's the bride."

"Great." Lorraine gestured to a lady standing behind her. "Priscilla will be your stylist. Come this way ladies."

Lorraine walked into the next room and pointed to the other beauticians. "The rest of you can choose whoever you want to do your hair and nails."

"I remember Sandra from the last time we were here." Cissy walked over to her and smiled. "I'm in your hands."

The rest of the bridal party chose who they wanted and sat in their appropriate chairs.

"What about our nails?" Becky inquired.

Lorraine pointed to the nail counter. "Choose whatever color you'd like. I suggest something which will blend with your gowns, or perhaps a French manicure."

Becky nodded. "I think, I'm going to have a French manicure."

"Me, too," Cissy chimed in.

Everyone nodded in agreement.

Missy smiled at them. "I was going to suggest it but wanted y'all to have what you wanted."

"We'll start with the mani/pedi, and then the hair." Lorraine smiled. "Anyone want something to drink? Champagne, wine, or water?"

"I would love some water." Missy laughed. "If I have champagne or wine now, I'd be too giddy to walk down the aisle later."

"Water sounds good to me, too," Cissy uttered as everyone else agreed.

"Okay, I'll be back in a few minutes with your drinks. Relax, enjoy being pampered, and let us make you gorgeous." Lorraine turned and left the room.

"This is so much fun." Cissy giggled.

"When did Ryan get home?" Dottie asked.

"He arrived two days ago." Missy placed her feet in the foot spa liquid in front of her. "I began to wonder if he'd make it home and was so relieved when he stood at my door."

"I heard her shriek all the way upstairs." Cissy grinned. "I knew it was Ryan."

"Having him home took some of the tension away." Missy waved to her sisters and Becky. "Having all of you here with me today is helping to calm me before I walk down the aisle."

"I was nervous at my wedding until Tyler took my hand at the altar," Gayle stated. "A peace came over me and I knew there wasn't anything to be anxious about."

"I'm not worried about my future now like I was at the time y'all came back into my life." Missy looked at each sister, smiling. "God's plan for my life is falling into place."

"Your new life begins today." Becky looked at her watch and said, "Or should I say in about two hours?"

Everyone giggled with excitement. They laughed, talked, and soon were ready to go to the church and change into their dresses for the wedding.

* * *

Missy stood in awe as she looked at herself in her wedding gown. *God gave me peace amid chaos over the last months, guiding my life when I didn't know where to go. I know God will continue to guide it. Thank you, Jesus, for getting me to this day.*

A knock on the door sent the ladies into a flurry of activity. Missy's bridesmaids picked up their bouquets and lined up to walk down the aisle. She marveled at the blessings God gave her.

The door opened, and Becky's mom entered closing the door behind her. "Are y'all ready? It's time to start."

Becky hurried to her mother and hugged her. "I think we're ready." She turned and looked at the sisters.

In unison the others said, "I'm ready."

Becky approached Missy. "How about you?"

"I'm as ready as I can be." Missy went to each of the bridesmaids, hugged them, and told them she loved them. The last one she hugged was Becky. Their hug lasted longer and then they looked at each other.

"Becky, you've been with me for so long." Missy smiled. "You're my best friend, hopefully, forever. I don't want our friendship to change. I look forward to when you are the bride, and I'm in your wedding like we talked about."

"You're my best friend, too. I'm eager to be the bride with you by my side." Becky looked at the sisters. "You can count on me to always be there for you no matter what our future holds, but now you have real sisters, so you'll never be alone."

"Yes, I know." Missy glanced at her sisters. "Isn't it wonderful?"

Becky nodded and choked up. "God provided for you when everything seemed lost."

Mrs. Thomas opened the door. "Time to start the processional."

After all the bridesmaids left the room, Missy stepped into the hallway and was met by Mr. Sims, her dad's lawyer. He cleared his throat. "Missy, I'm so honored you allowed me to stand in for your father. I'd promised your dad to look after you if something ever happened to him." He cleared his throat again. "So, if you are ready, I'll walk you down the aisle in his place."

"Thank you for asking me if you could stand in for my father. I couldn't bear the thought of walking down the aisle by myself. Now it feels like my father is by my side."

Glancing to the front of the church, she

watched as Becky and her sisters walked down the aisle. Daniel, Richard, and three of Ryan's friends as the other groomsmen stood beside her soon-to-be husband. Missy took a deep breath, slipped her hand under Mr. Sims' offered arm, and took her first step toward her new life as Mrs. Ryan Franklin — never to feel lonely again.

The End

9 781941 516492